LINEAR ALGEBRA

MAVEN BOOKS

LINEAR ALGEBRA

HUSSEÏN TEVFIK PACHA

MAVEN BOOKS

Chennai　　　Trichy　　　New Delhi

MAVEN BOOKS

This edition has been published in india by arrangement with Carson Books, UK

ISBN 978-93-5527-000-9   Maxwell Press

All rights reserved
Printed and bound in India   No. 44, Nallathambi Street,
Triplicane, Chennai 600 005

MJP 1192   © Publishers, 2023

Publisher :   C. Janarthanan

Publisher's Note

The legacy of a country is in its varied cultural heritage, historical literature, developments in the field of economy and science. The top nations in the world are competing in the field of science, economy and literature. This vast legacy has to be conserved and documented so that it can be bestowed to the future generation. The knowledge of this legacy is slowly getting perished in the present generation due to lack of documentation.

Keeping this in mind, the concern with retrospective acquiring of rare books has been accented recently by the burgeoning reprint industry. Maven Books is gratified to retrieve the rare collections with a view to bring back those books that were landmarks in their time.

In this effort, a series of rare books would be republished under the banner, "Maven Books". The books in the reprint series have been carefully selected for their contemporary usefulness as well as their historical importance within the intellectual. We reconstruct the book with slight enhancements made for better presentation, without affecting the contents of the original edition.

Most of the works selected for republishing covers a huge range of subjects, from history to anthropology. We believe this reprint edition will be a service to the numerous researchers and practitioners active in this fascinating field.

We allow readers to experience the wonder of peering into a scholarly work of the highest order and seminal significance.

Maven Books

CONTENTS.

CHAPTER I.

CHAPTER II.

CHAPTER III.

CHAPTER IV.

CHAPTER V.

LINEAR ALGEBRA

CHAPTER I.

1. The author here desires to say to the reader, that though the present chapter contains nothing new it is yet of unquestioned importance for a clear understanding of the chapters following.

2. If the lines A B, N O, for example, of a geometric figure are in different directions, and *if not only their absolute lengths are considered, but their respective directions as well*, it is evident that, though the lengths of these lines are equal, it cannot be said A B$=$N O.

3. By the expression A B$=$N O, in Linear Algebra and in the science of Quaternions also, it is understood that the length of A B is equal to that of N O, and also that the direction of the line A B is the same as that of N O, that is to say they are either on the same straight line or are parallel to each other in the same direction. But in Numerical Algebra it is the absolute equality of the lengths only of these lines which is understood.

4. In describing a line A B for example, if we say the line A B or simply A B we mean the special line A B which has a determined direction and length. If we write the line $\overline{AB}$, or simply $\overline{AB}$, we mean that the lenght alone is considered.

$\overline{\text{Sometimes}}$ I shall write N (A B) for $\overline{AB}$ and N (α), for $\underline{\alpha}$. I shall also write N² (A B), N² (α) for N(A B)$\times$N(A B), N(α)$\times$N(α), or for $\overline{AB}\times\overline{AB}$, $\alpha\times\alpha$. In these cases by the letter N prefixed to a line will be meant the number of the abstract length of that line.

5. To represent the different lines of a figure with regard to their directions as well as lengths, Greek letters are often employed. For example, if ρ is put for the line A B, so long as the problem is not changed, by this ρ is understood the line A B which by supposition has a determined length and direction.

6. It is obvious that the lines A B, B D, having a determined direction and length, the line A D will also, necessarily have a determined direction and length; and if in departing from the point A after having traced the line A B in giving to it its direction and length, we trace B D commencing at B, giving to it also its length and direction, the distance from A to D will represent the line A D with its special length and direction.

7. The operation of tracing the line A B from the point A, and the line B D from the point B, and giving to them their respective directions, will be represented by the expression A B+B D; and to show that by this operation A D is found, the expression A B+B D=A D will be employed.

8. If in departing from the point A the lines A B, B D, D H, H N, N O, are successively traced in their respective directions, the line joining A to O, or A O, will be represented by

$$A\,O=A\,B+B\,D+D\,H+N\,O.$$

It is readily seen that after having traced A B, if in place of tracing the other lines in the order given, we trace successively a line parallel and equal in length to each one of these lines, in their respective directions. in whatever order, we shall still find the same line A O.

It is needless to say that this manner of representation of straight lines is general.

9. It is now apparent what in Linear Algebra is meant by A B+B D=A D. If the lines A B, B D are found equal in length, it is evident the length of A D will diminish with the angle A B D; and finally A D will become zero whenever this angle does; in this case the point D coincides with A, and the line B D with B A; for this reason

$$A\,B+B\,D=0 \quad \text{or} \quad A\,B+B\,A=0.$$

Thus in the expressions

$$A\,B+B\,A \text{ or } B\,A+A\,B$$

A B and B A neutralize each other; therefore when a line measured in one direction is represented by a positive symbol, the same line measured in the opposite direction may be represented by the same symbol taken negatively, that is

$$A\,B=-B\,A \text{ or } B\,A=-A\,B,$$

hence if the line A B is represented by ρ, the line B A will be $-\rho$.

10. If A B, D E are on the same right line, and in the same direction, we admit, as in Numerical Algebra, that A B is to D E as $\underline{A\,B}$ to $\underline{D\,E}$, that is

$$A\,B=\frac{\underline{A\,B}}{\underline{D\,E}}\,D\,E.$$

Now if $\underline{A\,B}=\underline{D\,E}$, then A B=D E and consequently

$$A\,B+E\,D=0.$$

11. If A B, D E are parallel in the same direction, and $\underline{A\,B}=\underline{D\,E}$, we must admit

$$A\,B=D\,E.$$

For if we take A N, D M on the same right line A D, and A N=D M, we admit A N=D M (art. 10),

but D E compared to D M is situated exactly as A B compared to A N, and this similarity of position is so complete that if we know A B from its relation to A N it will be exactly as if we knew D E from its relation to D M. Therefore as D M is admitted to be equal to A M we have a right to assume that A B equals D E.

Thus
$$A B = D E \text{ and } A B + E D = 0.$$

And if
$$\underline{A F} = x. \underline{D G}$$

we shall have
$$A F = x. D G.$$

12. It follows that, If a line A B is represented by $a\alpha$ (a being an abstract number, α a unit line in the direction A B), any line which is parallel to A B or placed on the same line, and in the same direction and has the same length, can be designated also by $a\alpha$. In the case that the second line is in an opposite direction it will be designated by $-a\alpha$.

13. We have seen that A B, B D, D H drawn successively in their respective directions, the line A H which closes the polygon A B D H can be represented by

$$A H = A B + B D + D H,$$

or by designating the units of A B, B D, D H respectively by α, β, γ, and their lengths by x, y, z, and the line A H, by ρ, then

$$\rho = x\alpha + y\beta + z\gamma.$$

14. It is obvious that, if the lines A B, B D, D H are not in the same plane we can consider the numbers x, y and z as cartisian coordinates of the point H.

When the directions O X, O Y, O Z are perpendicular one to the other, we shall use often i, j, k to designate the linear units which are respectively in the directions O X, O Y, and O Z; if x, y, z represent the rectangular coordinates of a point and ρ the line which joins the origin O to this point, we shall have

$$\rho = x i + y j + z k.$$

ADDITION.

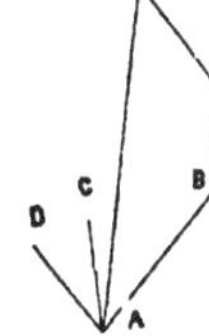

15. If we take the lines A B, A C, A D for example, and trace from the point B a line equal to A C, and from the end of this a line equal to A D and designate by A H the side which will close the polygon thus formed, the line A H will be called the *sum* of the lines A B, A G, A D, or

$$A H = A B + A C + A D.$$

This operation we define as *addition.*

It will also be readily seen that the following operations

$$A B + A D + A C,$$

$$A C + A B + A D,$$

$$A D + A C + A B \text{ etc.}$$

will give the same result. In the case in which the lines to be added are in the same direction, this operation is reduced to the addition of Numerical Algebra.

SUBTRACTION

16. Is the operation of finding one of two lines, when the other and their sum are given. To subtract A D from A B, or to find a line which added to A D will produce the line A B, it is evident that if we trace from the point B a line equal to D A, we shall have the line A N which added to A D will produce A B:

$$A N = A B - A D$$

and

$$A N + A D = A B.$$

A few propositions on the employment of lines in Algebraic operations.

17. In the case that we have

$$A B + B D + D H = A H$$

we shall have also

$$n \times A B + n \times B D + n \times D H = n \times A H,$$

in designating by n an abstract number. And if we have

$$n \times A B + n \times B D + n \times D H = n \times A H$$

we shall have

$$A B + B D + D H = A H.$$

In tracing the expressions $A B + B D + D H$, and $n \times A B + n \times B D + n \times D H$, the truth of the proposition will be manifest. Thus if we designate the lines A B, B D, D H, and H L by the Greek letters α, β, γ, δ, and if we have, for exemple,

$$28 \alpha + 21 \beta + 7 \gamma + 49 \delta = 14 \omega.$$

We shall have also as in Numerical Algebra

$$7 \, (4 \alpha + 3 \beta + \gamma + 7 \delta) = 7. \, 2 \omega$$

or

$$4 \alpha + 3 \beta + \gamma + 7 \delta = 2 \omega.$$

18. If the lines α, β have not the same direction, and we designate by a and b two abstract numbers, the lines $a \alpha$, $b \beta$ cannot neutralize each other in Algebraic expressions. Therefore if as a result of some operation we have,

$$a \alpha + b \beta = 0$$

we shall conclude that $a = 0$, $b = 0$.

And again if α and β being in different directions, we have

$$a\alpha + b\beta = k\alpha + l\beta$$

we must also have

$$(a - k)\alpha + (b - l)\beta = 0;$$

$$a - k = 0 \text{ and } b - l = 0.$$

19. If α, β, γ are non parallel lines in the same plane, it is always possible to find the numerical values of a, b, c, so that,

$$a\alpha + b\beta + c\gamma \text{ shall} = 0.$$

For as these α, β, and γ are on the same plane, a triangle can be constructed the sides of which shall be parallel respectively to α, β, γ. Now if the sides of this triangle taken in order be

$$a\alpha, \quad b\beta, \quad c\gamma$$

we shall have, by going around the triangle,

$$a\alpha + b\beta + c\gamma = 0.$$

20. If α, β, γ are three lines neither parallel, nor in the same plane, it is impossible to find numerical values of a, b, c, not equal to zero, which shall render $a\alpha + b\beta + c\gamma = 0$, for $a\alpha + b\beta$ can be represented by a line in the plane parallel to α, β. Now $c\gamma$ is not in that plane, therefore the sum of $a\alpha + b\beta$ and $c\gamma$ cannot equal 0. It follows that, if $a\alpha + b\beta + c\gamma = 0$ and α, β, γ are not parallel to each other, they are in the same plane.

21. There is but one way of making the sum of the multiples of α, β, γ equal to 0.

Let
$$a\alpha + b\beta + c\gamma = 0$$

and also
$$a_{,}\alpha + b_{,}\beta + c_{,}\gamma = 0.$$

By eliminating γ we get

$$(a c_{,} - c a_{,})\alpha + (b c_{,} - c b_{,})\beta = 0;$$

but as α, β are in different directions,

$$a c_{,} - c a_{,} = 0 \text{ and } b c_{,} - c b_{,} = 0;$$

$$a c_{,} = c a \quad \text{ and } b c_{,} = c b_{,}$$

or
$$a : b : c :: a_{,} : b_{,} : c_{,},$$

so that the second equation is simply a multiple of the first. If we observe that the triangles which give the different values of a, b, c, are similar the last proposition will be accepted *a priori*.

22. If α, β, γ are coinitial coplanar lines, terminating in a straight line, then the

same values of a, b, c which render $a\alpha + b\beta + c\gamma = 0$ will also render $a + b + c = 0$.

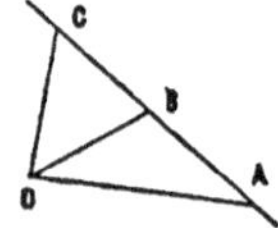

Let $\quad OA = \alpha,\ OB = \beta,\ OC = \gamma;$
then
$$AB = \beta - \alpha,$$
$$AC = \gamma - \alpha.$$

But AC is a multiple of AB, or

$$\gamma - \alpha = x(\beta - \alpha) = x\beta - x\alpha;$$

$$x\alpha - \alpha - x\beta + \gamma = 0,$$

or
$$(x-1)\alpha - x\beta + \gamma = 0;$$

and as in this equation the coefficients of α, β, γ are $x-1$, $-x$, $+1$ which correspond to a, b, c in the first equation, and as $(x-1) - x + 1 = 0$, then $a + b + c = 0$.

22. Conversely, if α, β, γ are coinitial, coplanar lines, and if both $a\alpha + b\beta + c\gamma = 0$, and $a + b + c = 0$, then do α, β, γ terminate in a straight line.

For by supposition,

$$a + b + c = 0,$$

therefore
$$a\gamma + b\gamma + c\gamma = 0,$$
and by subtraction
$$a(\gamma - \alpha) + b(\gamma - \beta) = 0$$

or
$$(\gamma - \alpha) + \frac{b}{a}(\gamma - \beta) = 0.$$

This shows that $\gamma - \alpha$ is a multiple of $\gamma - \beta$ and therefore it is in the same straight line with it; α, β, γ terminate in that straight line.

23. Examples.

Ex. 1. In a plane triangle are given one angle, an adjacent side, and the sum of the lengths of the other sides, to determine the triangle.

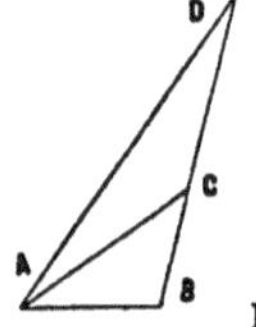

Let ABD be the given angle,

$AB = b\quad$,, ,, ,, side,

$S\qquad\quad$,, ,, sum of the lengths of the other two sides.

If in designating by α and β two unit lines, we represent by $x\alpha$ the unknown side adjacent to the angle B, and by $y\beta$ the opposite side to this angle, we shall have

$$y\beta = b + x\alpha$$

and
$$S = x + y,$$

by eliminating x

$$y\beta = b + S\alpha - y\alpha;$$

$$y\beta + y\alpha = b + S\alpha.$$

The last equation furnishes us a method of solution for this problem. For $S\alpha$ is known, and it represents the line BD which has the lengths S, the unit of this line being α; therefore $b + S\alpha$ or AD is known also; and $y\beta + y\alpha$ being equal to $b + S\alpha$ is equal to AD. But as α and β are units, AD, $y\beta$ and $y\alpha$ in the expression $AD = y\beta + y\alpha$ evidently form an isoceles triangle of which AD is the base, and $y\beta$, $y\alpha$ the equal sides (in lengths). Besides as α is a unit in the direction BD, the side $y\alpha$ must necessarily be in this direction. Thus evidently the angle BDA is one of the equal angles of that triangle. Then to find the other angle we have only to make an angle DAC equal to the angle BDA and thus we shall have $CD = y\alpha$ and $AC = y\beta$ which is the side opposite to the angle ABD in the demanded triangle.

Ex. 2. The difference between the diagonal of a square and one of its sides being given, to determine the square.

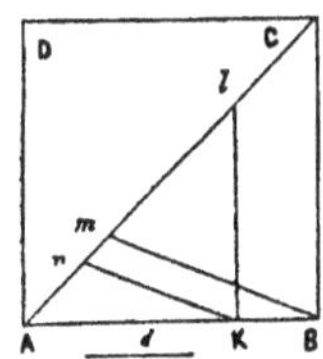

Let the difference between the length of the side AB and of the diagonal AC be d.

α, β, γ being three units, we will designate the side AB by $x\alpha$, the side BC by $x\beta$ and the diagonal AC by $y\gamma$, we shall now have,

$$y\gamma = x\alpha + x\beta,$$

$$y - x = d,$$

and from these two equations

$$x(\alpha + \beta - \gamma) = d\gamma.$$

The units α, β, γ in this equation are known, for if we put the unit α on the line AK and the unit β, perpendicularly upon α, the unit γ will be found on the $\alpha + \beta$. Therefore if we take $AK = \alpha$ and $Kl = \beta$ and $ln = -\gamma$, we shall have $An = \alpha + \beta - \gamma$, and in taking the length Am equal to the difference d, Am will be $= d\gamma$, and consequently

$$x \cdot An = Am.$$

But as An and Am are in the same direction we can say

$$x \cdot \underline{An} = \underline{Am},$$

$$x = \frac{\underline{Am}}{\underline{An}}.$$

Therefore it is evident that in joining the points n and K, and tracing the line mB parallel to nK we shall have

$$\frac{\underline{Am}}{\underline{An}} = \frac{\underline{AB}}{\underline{AK}} \quad \text{or as} \quad \underline{AK} = 1,$$

$$\frac{\underline{A\,m}}{\underline{A\,n}} = \underline{A\,B},$$

$$x = \underline{A\,B}$$

which is the length of the side of the demanded square.

Ex. 3. The bisectors of the sides of a triangle meet in a point which trisects each of them.

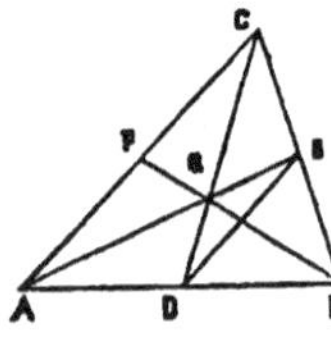

Let the sides of the triangle A B C be bisected in D, E, F and let A E and C D meet in G; it will be seen that the line D E is parallel to A C and that it is the half of it.

Therefore,

$$A\,G + G\,C = A\,C = 2(D\,G + G\,E) = 2\,D\,G + 2\,G\,E;$$

$$(A\,G - 2\,G\,E) + (G\,C - 2\,D\,G) = 0.$$

But as $A\,G - 2\,G\,E$ is on the line A E, $GC - 2\,D\,G$ on the line C D, their sum cannot be zero unless each one of them equals zero.
Consequently,

$$A\,G - 2\,G\,E = 0, \text{ or } A\,G = 2\,G\,E,$$

and

$$G\,C - 2\,D\,G = 0, \text{ or } G\,C = 2\,D\,G.$$

These equations show that E G is a third of E A and D G a third of D C.

If now we suppose that the point G is the point where C D and B F meet, in the same manner it will be seen that D G is a third of D C, and F G a third of F B, and consequently the three bisectors must necessarily meet in the same point which separates one third of each.

Ex. 4. The middle points of the lines which join the points of bisection of the opposite sides of a quadrilateral, coincide, whether the four sides of the quadrilateral be in the same plane or not.

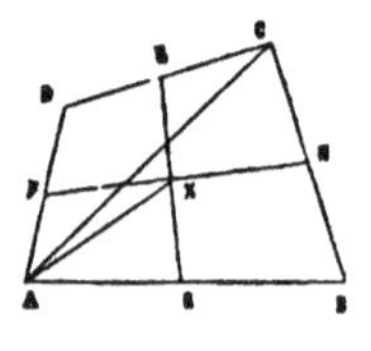

Let $A\,B = \alpha$, $A\,C = \beta$, $A\,D = \gamma$,

X the middle point of E G.

We have

$$A\,E + E\,G = A\,D + D\,G,$$

$$\tfrac{1}{2}\alpha + E\,G = \gamma + \tfrac{1}{2}(\beta - \gamma);$$

$$E\,G = \gamma + \tfrac{1}{2}(\beta - \gamma) - \tfrac{1}{2}\alpha = \tfrac{1}{2}(\beta + \gamma - \alpha),$$

and as

$$A\,X = \tfrac{1}{2}\alpha + \tfrac{1}{2}E\,G,$$

$$A\,X = \tfrac{1}{2}\alpha + \tfrac{1}{4}(\beta + \gamma - \alpha) = \tfrac{1}{4}(\alpha + \beta + \gamma)$$

which being symmetrical in α, β, γ is the same for the line from A to the middle of H F, hence the middle points of the lines E G, F H must coincide.

Being naturally desirous to publish this little work as economically as may prove compatible with clearness of statement, I have contented myself with putting into the present chapter some readily solved examples only. Should however any one wish further illustration, he can find very beautiful and sufficiently difficult solutions of a similar kind in the second chapter of the Introduction to Quaternious by Kelland and Tait.

CHAPTER II.

MULTIPLICATION.

24. One of the various directions will be considered as the *principal direction*. In the following Figure O X is assumed to be such a direction.

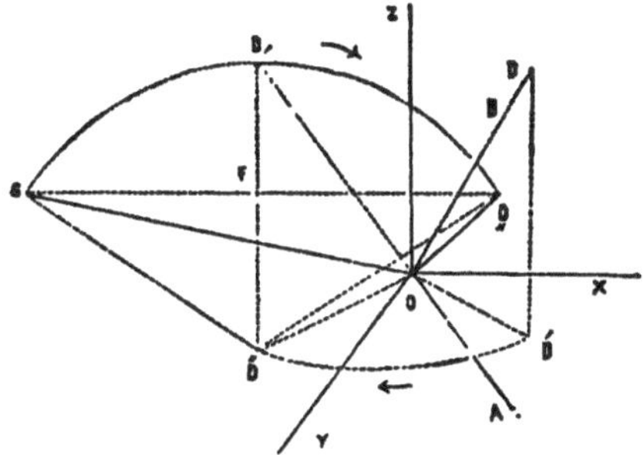

The *multiplication* of one by the other of any two coinitial lines not in the same plane with the principal direction, is shown in the following operation.

Suppose we want to find the *product* of the line O B by O A.

1st. Put upon the direction O B the product of the line O B by the abstract number which is the ratio of the line O A to its unit; and suppose this product is O D.

2nd. Let down a perpendicular from the point D on the plane which passes through the principal direction O X and the line O A.

Let D' be the foot of this perpendicular in the same plane. We thus have a rectangular triangle whose plane is perpendicular to the indefinite plane X O A, of which D D' is the hight; O D' the base, O D the hypothenuse.

3d. Move this triangle around the point O keeping it always perpendicular to the plane X O A until its base O D', comes on O D" which is on the aforesaid plane, and which makes with OX an angle equal to the sum of the angles that OD' and OA, make with the principal direction OX. Let D,D'' be the hight of this triangle after this operation.

For definiteness we will admit that the angles which the lines OA and OD' make with the principal direction are formed and measured from OX on this side. That is, to form these angles with the principal direction, the lines OA and OD' are assumed to have made on the indefinite plane XOA a rotation similar to that of the hands of a watch.

4th. Let us imagine that a plane parallel to the principal direction passes through the hight D,D'', and that on this plane the line D,D'' turns from left to right around the point D'' also like the hands of a watch as much as the angle $D_{,,}D''D$, between the new position and $D''D$, shall be equal to the angle AOX that the line OA makes with the principal direction.

Now the line $OD_{,,}$, which joins the point O to the point $D_{,,}$ is the required *product* of OB by OA.

25. We shall see that the results of this *multiplication* have a great analogy with the results of ordinary multiplication, which in fact is but a particular case of it. Consequently we shall use the same signs that are used in Numerical Algebra. Thus in designating OA, OB, $OD_{,,}$ respectively by α, β, γ, we shall write as in Numerical Algebra

$$\alpha \times \beta \quad \text{or} \quad \alpha \cdot \beta \quad \text{or} \quad \alpha\beta = \gamma.$$

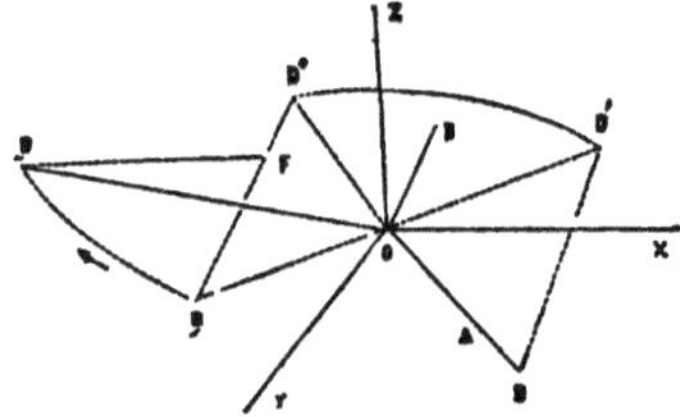

26. Had we wished to *multiply* OA by OB we should have had the same operation to make which we have just written, with this single change, that the plane XOB would have had to be taken instead of the plane XOA, and the line OA instead of the line OB.

27. It is readily seen that the *product* of OB by OA is not generally the same as the *product* of AO by OB. Thus we cannot ordinarily say $\alpha \cdot \beta = \beta \cdot \alpha$; that is the *commutative* law does not ordinarily apply to the *factors of a linear product*. This law, as we shall soon see, is a property of a special case of General Multiplication.

28. Let $D_{,,}F$ be parallel to XO (Fig. art. 24), consequently perpendicular to D,D''. It is uselful to know the value of this line $D_{,,}F$.

Let us suppose that φ indicates the angle AOX; ω, the angle DOD' which is between OD and its projection in the plane XOA. Since the angle $D_{,,}D''D$, is equal to the angle AOX (art. 24), we have

$$\underline{D_{,,}F} = \underline{D_{,,}D''} \cdot \operatorname{Sin}\,\varphi;$$

but

$$\underline{D_{,,}D''} = \underline{D,D''} = \underline{DD'},$$

therefore

$$\underline{D_{,,}F} = \underline{DD'} \cdot \operatorname{Sin}\,\varphi;$$

but
$$\underline{D\,D'} = \underline{O\,D}\,.\,\text{Sin }\omega = \underline{O\,A}\,.\,\underline{O\,B}\,.\,\text{Sin }\omega,$$

consequently
$$\underline{D_{\prime\prime}\,F} = \underline{O\,A}\,.\,\underline{O\,B}\,.\,\text{Sin }\varphi\,.\,\text{Sin }\omega,$$

or
$$F\,D_{\prime\prime} = \underline{O\,A}\,.\,\underline{O\,B}\,.\,\text{Sin }\varphi\,.\,\text{Sin }\omega\,.\,i,$$

i being the unity of length in the principal direction $O\,X$.

29. If the question was of the product $O\,B \times O\,A$ (art. 26), $F\,D_{\prime\prime}$ would have been directed in the opposite direction to $O\,X$ and we would have

$$F\,D_{\prime\prime} = -\,\underline{O\,B}\,.\,\underline{O\,A}\,.\,\text{Sin }\Phi\,.\,\text{Sin }\psi\,.\,i,$$

Φ being the angle $B\,O\,X$; ψ the angle which is between $O\,A$ and its projection in the plane $X\,O\,B$.

It is easy to see that if θ indicates the angle which is between the planes $X\,O\,A$, $X\,O\,B$, we shall have

$$\text{Sin }\omega = \text{Sin }\Phi\,.\,\text{Sin }\theta,$$

$$\text{Sin }\psi = \text{Sin }\varphi\,.\,\text{Sin }\theta.$$

Rule of Signs.

30. Algebraists have laboriously attempted to demonstrate that

$$a \times -b = -a\,b,\quad -a \times b = -a\,b \text{ and}$$

$$-a \times -b = +a\,b.$$

Nevertheless the demonstrations given in books of Numerical Algebra on this matter are not rigorously logical. This need not appear strange. The definitions given for multiplication are much less general than is the idea of a negative quantity. If therefore in employing only such definitions as are applicable to abstract numbers, algebraists have not succeeded in satisfactorily demonstrating the rules of signs as above stated, it is not to be wondered at.

31. To perceive that,

$$\alpha \times -\beta = -\alpha\beta,\quad -\alpha \times \beta = -\alpha\beta,\text{ and } -\alpha \times -\beta = \alpha\beta$$

we have merely to apply our definition.

Special cases of Linear Multiplication.

32. If $O\,B$ (Fig. art. 24) is perpendicular to the plane which passes through $O\,X$ and $O\,A$, the foot D' of the hight $D\,D'$ and the foot D'' of the hight $D_{\prime}\,D''$ will coincide with the origin O; consequently the lines $D''D_{\prime}$, $D''D_{\prime\prime}$ and $O\,D_{\prime\prime}$ will be found upon the plane which passes through $O\,X$ and $O\,B$, and at the same time the lines $O\,D_{\prime\prime}$ and $D''D_{\prime\prime}$ will coincide with each other.

In such a case the multiplication of $O\,B$ by $O\,A$ consists in turning upon the plane

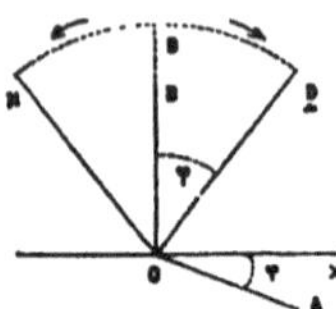

X O B form left to right the line O D, which is the product of O B by the abstract number of the length of O A, until the angle $D_{,,}OB$ shall be equal to the angle A O X $=\varphi$. O $D_{,,}$ is the required *product*.

It is readily seen that in this case, to find the product O B . O A, it is only necessary to turn O D to the opposite side; the required *product* will be O H, if the angle H O B $=\varphi$.

33. If the line O A is perpendicular to the plane X O B at the same time that O B is perpendicular, as in the preceding case to the plane X O A, or in other terms, if the lines O A, O B and the principal direction O X (Fig. art. 32) form the three contiguous sides of a rectangular parallelopiped, the angle $D O D_{,,}$ will be a right angle, and consequently the line O $D_{,,}$ which is the *product* of O B by O A will be found in the principal direction O X.

If in this case the required *product* is O B . O A, this *production* will evidently fall on the direction opposite to O X, that is to say on the negative principal direction.

34. Thus we have this important result, that when O A, O B and the principal direction are perpendicular to each other, in designating O A by α and O B by β we shall have

$$\alpha\beta=-\beta\alpha \quad \text{or} \quad \alpha\beta+\beta\alpha=0.$$

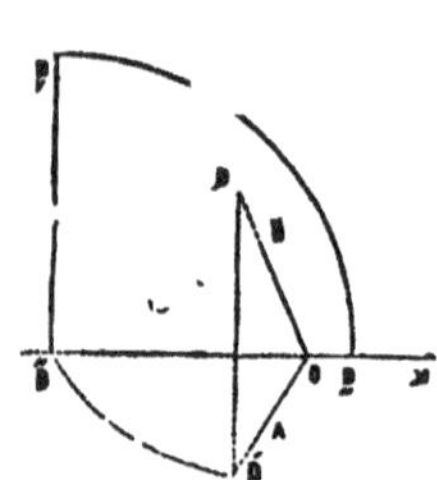

35. Let O A, OB be perpendicular to the principal direction O X, without that O A be perpendicular to O B; let us indicate by θ the angle B O A. In this case the point D' (Fig. Art. 24) is on the direction O A; D", on the opposite direction of O X; $D_{,,}$, on the direction D" X; and we shall have

$$D''O=D'O=OA . OB . \cos\theta,$$

$$D''D_{,,}=D'D''=DD'=OA . OB . \sin\theta;$$

consequently

$$OA \times OB = O D_{,,} = D''D_{,,} - D''O$$

$$=OA . OB . \sin\theta . i - OB . OA . \cos\theta . i$$

$$=OA . OB . (\sin\theta - \cos\theta) . i.$$

We shall have also

$$OB \times OA = -OB . OA . (\sin\theta + \cos\theta) . i \quad \text{(Art. 26.)}.$$

From these two relations we shall have

$$OA \times OB - OB \times OA = 2OA . OB . \sin\theta . i;$$

therefore in supposing that O A, O B, be two unities of length carried in the directions O A, O B; and in indicating them by β, $\beta_{,}$, we shall have

$$\beta\beta_{,} - \beta_{,}\beta = 2\sin\theta . i.$$

A curious result. If in the preceding case we have $\theta=\frac{\pi}{4}$, we must have

$$O\,A \times O\,B = 0,$$

a *product* which is naught when neither of its two factors are not so.

36. If the lines O A, O B and the principal direction O X (Art. 24) are in the same plane, the hight D D′ will be reduced to zero, and at the same time the point D″ will coincide with the point D″, and the line O D″ with the line O D″. We thus see that, when O A and O B and the principal direction are in the same plane, the *production* O A . O B will also be on the same plane and it will make with the principal direction an angle e-qual to the sum of the angles which O A and O B make with the principal direction. It is almost unnecessary to add that the *product* of O A by O B is the same as O A . O B. Thus in this specified case, we have as in Numerical Algebra $\alpha . \beta = \beta . \alpha$.

37. Let us designate by φ the angle which a line O A makes with the principal direction O X, and suppose that a line O B which is found on the same plane as O A and O X makes with this O X an angle equal to $2\pi - \varphi$. The production of these O A and O B will be found on the principal direction, that is to say,

$$O\,A . O\,B \text{ or } O\,B . O\,A = \underline{O\,A} . \underline{O\,B} . i;$$

this is a result of great importance in Linear Algebra.

38. If the lines O A, O B are on the same straight line, and in the same direction, they will necessarily be in the same plane as the principal direction, and the angle which their *production* makes with this direction (Art. 36) will be the double of the angle which their direction makes with the principal direction. And in the same supposition, the production of O A . O B and of a line O D which has the same direction as O A and O B, will be found also in the same plane, and will make an angle three times greater than the angle which the directions O A and O B make with the principal direction. The generality of this fact is evident.

39. It follows from the preceding case that if the direction of these lines O A and O B is perpendicular to the principal direction, their *production* will fall on the *negative principal direction*.

40. The *product* of a line by itself will be called the *square* of this line; the pro-duct of the square of a line by the line itself, its *cube*. It follows from Art. 38 that the square, the cube and the other powers of a line O A will be found in the same plane, as this line O A and the principal direction O X; and that the angles which the square, the cube and the other powers of this line make with the principal direction will be res-pectively twice, thrice and so forth greater than the angle which this line makes with the same direction.

41. To indicate the different *powers* of a line we shall employ the same mode used in Numerical Algebra. The square of O A $= (O\,A)^2$, the cube of O A $= (O\,A)^3$, or the square of $\alpha = \alpha^2$, the cube of $\alpha = \alpha^3$ and so on.

If δ is a unit perpendicular to the principal direction, and if i is the unit in this di-rection (Art. 39)

$$\delta^2 = -i, \quad \delta^3 = -\delta, \quad \delta^4 = i, \quad \delta^5 = \delta, \quad \delta^6 = -i.$$

We now know that the angle which α^5, for example, makes with the principal di-rection is five times greater than the angle that α makes with the same direction.

42. It results also from Art. 40 that if the units α and β are in the same plane with the principal direction, and that the angle which α makes with this direction is represented by θ, the angle which β makes with the same direction by φ, and lastly $\frac{\varphi}{\theta}$ or $\frac{\theta}{\varphi}$ represents but the ratio between the number of the degrees of these angles θ and φ, we shall have

$$\beta = \alpha^{\frac{\varphi}{\theta}} \quad \text{or} \quad \alpha = \beta^{\frac{\theta}{\varphi}},$$

or if $\theta =$ one degree

$$\beta = \alpha^{\varphi} \quad \text{and} \quad \alpha = \beta^{\frac{1}{\varphi}}.$$

Here φ represents the ratio of the angle φ to an angle of 1 degree which α is supposed to make with the principal direction.

43. If the lines β, δ and a unit α are on the same plane as the principal direction, and if the angles which these β, δ and α make with the principal direction are respectively θ, φ and one degree, and the lengths of β is b; that of δ, d; we shall have thus (Art. 42)

$$\beta = b\,\alpha^{\theta}, \quad \delta = d\,\alpha^{\varphi}$$

$$\beta \cdot \delta \text{ or } \delta \cdot \beta = b\,\alpha^{\theta} \times d\,\alpha^{\varphi} = b\,d\,\alpha^{\theta + \varphi}.$$

44. It is scarcely necessary to say that when $\delta^{2} = -i$, this δ could represent each one of the linear units which are perpendicular to the principal direction. If in using the sign $\sqrt{}$ we employ $\sqrt{-i}$ to represent one of these innumerable units, and if we adopt again a sign to represent another one, we should be able to represent not only each one of these others, but also a linear unit which may be found in any direction.

45. The unit of the principal direction being i, we shall make use of $\sqrt{-i}$ to represent the unit of a direction OY which is perpendicular to the principal direction OX, and we shall adopt the sign $\perp$ to represent the unit of the direction OZ which is perpendicular to the plane XOY. Thus we can write (Arts. 13, 14.)

$$\rho = x\,i + y\sqrt{-i} + z\,\perp.$$

We must bear in mind that according to our definition of *Multiplication*,

$$(\sqrt{-i})^{2} = -i, \quad (\perp)^{2} = -i \text{ (Art 41)},$$

and
$$\sqrt{-i} \times \perp = +i, \quad \perp \times \sqrt{-i} = -i \text{ (Art. 33)}.$$

46. If $X = 0$ then $\rho = y\sqrt{-i} + z\,\perp$ will represent a line perpendicular to the principal direction, and if $z = 0$, then $\rho = x\,i + y\sqrt{-i}$ will represent a line situated on the plane XOY.

47. If the line OA is in the principal direction (Art. 24) the plane XOA will become indeterminate. But in taking it in no matter what position, it will be seen that $OD_{\shortparallel}$ will always coincide with OD. Therefore in this case $OA \cdot OB = OB \cdot OA = OD$.

If follows therefore that if the absolute length of $OB = b$, the unit of $OB = \beta$, and the principal unit $= i$

$$OB = b\beta = i \times b\beta = bi \times \beta = \beta \times bi = b\beta \times i.$$

And
$$\beta = i\beta = \beta i;$$

$b\beta$ represents β added b times to itself; and $bi \times \beta$ or $\beta \times bi$, represents β multiplied by bi, or bi multiplied by β.

48. If O A and O B are both in the principal direction, their product will also be found in the principal direction.

Therefore
$$i \times i = i \text{ and } i \times i \times i = i \text{ etc.}$$

49. Hence we see that the units and the lines found on the principal direction have the same properties as the ordinary units and numbers represented by lines. Besides, in the results which we find whether by addition, subtraction or multiplication no absolute or abstract term enters. Therefore if in our calculations we replace the principal unit i by 1 no complication or mistake can arise, but on the contrary a great simplicity in the calculation will result from it.

Thus, we can write (Art. 45)

$$\rho = x + y \,|\!\sqrt{-1} + z \perp;$$

in this case

$$(\sqrt{-1})^2 = -1, \quad (\perp)^2 = -1,$$

and
$$\sqrt{-1}\perp = 1, \quad \perp\sqrt{-1} = -1.$$

50. To show the manner of linear multiplication of two lines, we have supposed them *coinitial*; nevertheless to apply our definition of multiplication to any two lines whatever, it is merely required to add to this definition the following. To multiply a line Q R by a line M N, it is necessary to trace from the point M a line equal to Q R (Arts. 3, 11) or from the point Q a line equal to M N. The definition will be applied to the line M N and to the equal of O R which passes through M or to the line Q R with the equal of M N which passes through Q. We can readily convince ourselves that the line which represents the production of the line M N by the equal of Q R which passes through M is equal (Arts. 3, 11) to the line which represents the production of the equal of M N passing through Q by O R. This line will be found equal to the line which will represent the production of these lines M N and Q R transposed to any common origin O, without changing their respective directions. It is clearly understood that in all of these three multiplications the principal directions must be the same.

Multiplication of Polynominals.

51. It now remains to be shown that, α and β being transposed to the same origin (Art. 50) if in α, β we put $\alpha = \gamma + \delta$, and $\beta = \lambda + \mu$, that is to say, if the lines α and β are each the sum of two other lines, we shall have as in numerical algebra

$$(\gamma + \delta) . (\lambda + \mu) = \gamma . \lambda + \delta . \lambda + \gamma . \mu + \delta . \mu.$$

52. Let us commence by proving that,

$$O A . O M + O A . O N = O A . (O M + O N) = O A . O B,$$

O B being the sum of O M and O N.

We readily perceive, that after having multiplied O M, O N and O B by the abstract number of the length of O A, the extremities of these products and the origin O will form a parallelogram, as well as the extremities of O M, O N, O B and the origin O. The feet of the perpendiculars, let fall according to the definition (Art. 24) on the plane which passes through the principal direction and O A, also form with the said origin, a parallelogram. Thus we are able to show that the extremities of the productions O A . O B, O A . O M, O A . O N, and the origin O must form a parallelogram whose diagonal and two sides contiguous to the point O, are respectively O A . O B, O A . O M and O A . O N. Therefore

$$O A . O B = O A . O M + O A . O N$$

or

$$O A . (O M + O N) = O A . O M + O A . O N.$$

53. Let us show now that

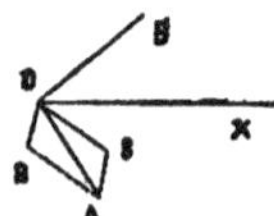

$$O R . O B + O S . O B = (O R + O S) . O B = O A . O B,$$

O A being the sum of O R and O S. Let us suppose for the moment that O R, O S are found in the plane X O A.

In this case also we shall easily see that the extremities of the products O S . O B, O A . O B, O R . O B and the origin O form a parallelogram, the diagonal of which starting from O is O A . O B and the two sides starting from the said point O are O R . O B, O S . O B. Therefore

$$O A . O B = O R . O B + O S . O B,$$

or

$$(O R + O S) . O B = O R . O B + O S . O B.$$

54. It results from the preceding two propositions that if O R, O S are found in the same plane as the principal direction, we shall have

$$(O R + O S) (O M + O N)$$

$$= (O R + O S) O M + (O R + O S) O N$$

$$= O R . O M + O S . O M + O R . O N + O S . O N.$$

55. Let O A, O B be two lines whatever in the space (Eig. Art. 24) and let us suppose

$$O A = x i + y \beta,$$

$$O B = x_, i + y_, \beta_,,$$

β, $\beta_,$, being two unities of lengths perpendicular to the principal direction, in which the unity of length is represented by i (Art. 28); x, y, the projections of O A on the principal direction and on that of β; $x_,$, $y_,$, the projections of O B on the principal direction and on that of β. It is evident that β is in the plane X O A; $\beta_,$, in the plane X O B;

and the angle which is between β, β, measures the dihedral angle which these two planes form. Therefore according to the last proposition we shalle have

$$OA \times OB = (x\,i + y\,\beta)\,(x_,i + y_,\beta_,)$$

$$= x\,x_,\,i^2 + y\,x_,\beta\,i + x\,y_,\,i\beta_, + y\,y_,\beta\beta_,$$

$$= x\,x_,\,i + y\,x_,\beta + x\,y_,\beta_, + y\,y_,\beta\beta_,\ (\text{Arts. } 47, 48).$$

We shall have also, by multiplying OA by OB (Art. 26),

$$OB \times OA = (x_,i + y_,\beta_,)\,(x\,i + y\,\beta)$$

$$= x_,\,x\,i + y_,\,x\,\beta_, + x_,\,y\,\beta + y_,\,y\,\beta_,\beta\ (\text{Arts. } 47, 48),$$

consequently

$$OA \times OB - OB \times OA = y\,y_,(\beta\beta_, - \beta_,\beta),$$

or

$$OA \times OB = OB \times OA + y\,y_,(\beta\beta_, - \beta_,\beta).$$

Let θ be the angle which is between β, $\beta_,$; Φ, the angle BOX; φ, the angle AOX. Therefore

$$y = \underline{OA}\,.\,\text{Sin }\varphi,\ \ y_, = \underline{OB}\,\text{Sin }\Phi,$$

and

$$\beta\beta_, - \beta_,\beta = 2\,\text{Sin }\theta\,.\,i\ (\text{Art. } 35),$$

consequently

$$OA \times OB = OB \times OA + 2\underline{OA}\,.\,\underline{OB}\,.\,\text{Sin }\Phi\,.\,\text{Sin }\varphi\,.\,\text{Sin }\theta\,.\,i,$$

We have already seen that (Arts. 28, 29)

$$\underline{OA} \times \underline{OB}\,.\,\text{Sin }\varphi\,.\,\text{Sin }\Phi\,.\,\text{Sin }\theta\,.\,i = FD_{,,},$$

or by taking $GF = FD_{,,}$ (Fig. Art. 24),

$$GD_{,,} = 2\underline{OA}\,.\,\underline{OB}\,.\,\text{Sin }\Phi\,.\,\text{Sin }\varphi\,.\,\text{Sin }\theta\,.\,i.$$

Therefore

$$OA \times OB = OB \times OA + GD_{,,}.$$

56. This last relation shows that to have the product $OB \times OA$ (Art. 26), we could act exactly as if we would want to find $OA \times OB$ (Art. 24), with the only change that instead of turning $D''D$, from left to right through the angle AOX, it would be necessary to turn it from right to left again the angle AOX. Thus we should have

$$OG = OB \times OA.$$

57. Now let $OA = OS + OR$, without that OR, OS, be found in the same plane with OX. We have already seen that (Art. 52)

$$OB \times OA = OB \times (OR + OS)$$

$$= OB\,.\,OR + OB\,.\,OS.$$

Let us indicate by ω the angle that O A makes by its projection in the plane X O B; by μ and ν, the angles that O R, O S, make respectively with their projections in the same plane. Therefore (Art. 55)

$$O B \times O A = O A \times O B - 2 \underline{O A} \cdot \underline{O B} \cdot \text{Sin}\,\omega \cdot \text{Sin}\,\Phi \cdot i,$$

$$O B \times O R = O R \times O B - 2 \underline{O R} \cdot \underline{O B} \cdot \text{Sin}\,\mu \cdot \text{Sin}\,\Phi \cdot i,$$

$$O B \times O S = O S \times O B - 2 \underline{O S} \cdot \underline{O B} \cdot \text{Sin}\,\nu \cdot \text{Sin}\,\Phi \cdot i;$$

and by substitution we shall have

$$O A \times O B \text{ or } (O R + O S) \times O B$$

$$= O R \cdot O B + O S \cdot O B;$$

because the perpendiculars running down from A, R, S, to the plane X O B are respectively

$$\underline{O A} \cdot \text{Sin}\,\omega, \quad \underline{O R} \cdot \text{Sin}\,\mu, \quad \underline{O S} \cdot \text{Sin}\,\nu;$$

and by a well-known theorem

$$\underline{O A}\ \text{Sin}\,\omega = \underline{O R} \cdot \text{Sin}\,\mu + \underline{O S} \cdot \text{Sin}\,\nu$$

or

$$\underline{O A} \cdot \underline{O B} \cdot \text{Sin}\,\Phi \cdot \text{Sin}\,\omega \cdot i$$

$$= \underline{O R} \cdot \underline{O B} \cdot \text{Sin}\,\Phi \cdot \text{Sin}\,\mu \cdot i + \underline{O S} \cdot \underline{O B} \cdot \text{Sin}\,\Phi \cdot \text{Sin}\,\nu \cdot i.$$

58.   Let in general

$$O A = O R + O S,$$

$$O B = O M + O N.$$

Therefore

$$O A \times (O M + O N) = O A \times O M + O A \times O N \text{ (Art. 52)};$$

$$O A \times O M + O A \times O N$$

$$= (O R + O S)\, O M + (O R + O S)\, O N$$

$$= O R \cdot O M + O S \cdot O M + O R \cdot O N + O S \cdot O N \text{ (Art. 57)}.$$

Therefore, whatever may be the positions of the planes R O S, M O N, relating to the principal direction, we shall have as in numerical algebra,

$$(O R + O S)\ (O M + O N)$$

$$= O R \times O M + O S \times O M + O R \times O N + O S \times O N,$$

expression which indicates the manner to multiply a binomial by a binomial. It is easy to apply this rule to the multiplication of a polynominal whatever by a polynominal whatever,

Reverse of Multiplication.

59. We have seen (Fig. Art. 24) that $OD_{\prime\prime}$ is the product of OB by OA. Now let us suppose that the lines $OD_{\prime\prime}$ and OA being given, we want to find a line which, multiplied by OA will produce $OD_{\prime\prime}$. This is Reverse of Multiplication. The figure of Art. 24 shows how this inverse operation should be performed to find the required factor, which in this figure is OB. In some particular cases, for example, in the case where the given lines $OD_{\prime\prime}$, OA and the principal direction OX are in the same plane, and the angle XOA is equal to $\frac{\pi}{3}$, we shall find by this inverse operation certain different lines, each one of which if multiplied by the given factor will produce the given product; and but one of these factors will be in the plane which passes through the principal direction and the given multiplier, the others which are innumerable are on another plane which passes through the factor which is in the plane of the principal direction and of the given multiplier. Consequently, if we have $\alpha . \beta = \alpha . \beta$, for example, it would not in general be correct to conclude that $\beta = \beta_{,}$.

60. We see that we shall be able to have a relation such as $\alpha . \beta = \alpha . \beta_{,,}$ without that the equality $\beta = \beta_{,}$ may take place. Therefore from the equality

$$\alpha . \beta = \alpha . \beta_{,}$$

we shall have

$$\alpha . \beta - \alpha \beta_{,} = 0 \text{ or } \alpha (\beta - \beta_{,}) = 0 \text{ (Art. 52)};$$

therefore if

$$\beta - \beta_{,} = \delta,$$

$$\alpha . \delta = 0;$$

see Art. 35.

Conjugates.

61. When any two points A and B are on a line perpendicular to the principal direction, and are on different sides of this direction, and are equidistant from it, we shall term A a *Conjugate* of B and B a conjugate of A. We shall also term any line MN the conjugate of the line PQ and vice-versa whenever the point M is the conjugate of the point P and the point N of the point Q. In this case the lines MN and PQ will be of equal lengths.

We shall designate the conjugate of a line MN, for exemple, by $(MN)'$ and the conjugates of α, β, δ etc. by α', β', δ' etc.

62. Conformably to the definition of the addition of two lines (Art. 15) we shall have

$$\alpha + \alpha' = 2 \underline{\alpha} . \text{Cos } \varphi . i,$$

φ being the angle which is between a line whatever α and the principal direction.

63. The product of a line and its conjugate will be on the principal direction. For if from the origin O which is on the principal direction, we draw two lines respectively equal to given line and its conjugate, these two lines will be found in the same plane as the principal direction, and if one of them make with this direction, an angle φ, the other will make with the same direction an angle $2\pi - \varphi$; consequently this product, (Art. 37)

will be on the principal direction. The length of this product will be equal to the square of the length of the line given.

64. Thus in designating this line and its conjugate respectively by α and α', and its length by $\underline{\alpha}$, we shall have $\alpha \cdot \alpha'$ or $\alpha' \cdot \alpha = \underline{\alpha}^2 i$.

If we replace i by 1 (Art. 49),

$$\alpha \alpha' \quad \text{or} \quad \alpha' \alpha = \underline{\alpha}^2 .$$

65. *A theorem very important.* If we represent by α' the conjugate of α; by β', the conjugate of β; by $\underline{\alpha}$ and $\underline{\beta}$ the lengths of α and β (Art. 4); and lastly by θ the angle which is between α and β transferred to the same origin, we shall have

$$\alpha \beta' + \beta \alpha' = 2 \underline{\alpha} \underline{\beta} \, \text{Cos } \theta \cdot i.$$

For, let O X be the principal direction, $OA = \alpha$, $OB = \beta$, $AB = \delta$; $OA' = \alpha'$ and $OB' = \beta'$; it is evident that $A'B' = \delta'$ will be the conjugate of $AB = \delta$ and the angle $AOB = \theta$ will be equal to the angle $A'OB'$. Designate respectively the lengths of the lines O A, O B and A B by a, b and d . We shall have (Art. 16)

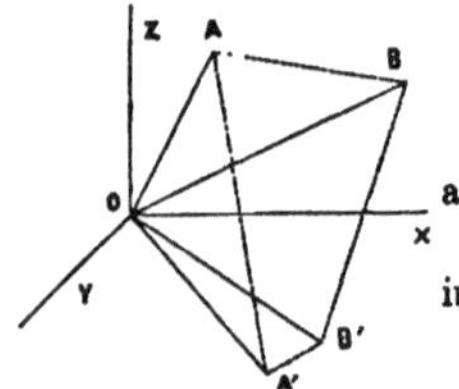

$$\delta = \beta - \alpha$$

and

$$\delta' = \beta' - \alpha';$$

in multiplying these two equalities by each other (Art. 58)

we shall have

$$\delta \delta' = \beta \beta' - \alpha \beta' - \beta \alpha' + \alpha \alpha' = \beta \beta' + \alpha \alpha' - (\alpha \beta' + \beta \alpha')$$

or

$$\alpha \beta' + \beta \alpha' = \beta \beta' + \alpha \alpha' - \delta \delta'.$$

But we know that (Art. 64)

$$\delta \delta' = d^2 \, i, \quad \beta \beta' = b^2 \, i, \quad \text{and} \quad \alpha \alpha' = a^2 \, i,$$

$$\alpha \beta' + \beta \alpha' = (a^2 + b^2 - d^2) \, i. \tag{1}$$

Therefore, if O A is taken as the principal direction, we shall have $\alpha = \alpha'$, $\beta \alpha' = a \beta$, $\alpha \beta' = a \beta'$ (Art. 47), and

$$\beta \alpha' + \alpha \beta' = a \, (\beta + \beta') = 2 \, ab \, \text{Cos } \varphi \cdot i,$$

φ being the angle A O B; therefore

$$(a^2 + b^2 - d^2) \, i = 2 \, a \, b \, \text{Cos } \varphi \cdot i,$$

or

$$a^2 + b^2 - d^2 = 2 \, a \, b \, \text{Cos } \varphi,$$

consequently

$$\alpha \beta' + \beta \alpha' = 2 \, ab \, \text{Cos } \varphi \cdot i \tag{2}$$

$$- 23 -$$

If
$$\theta = \frac{\pi}{2},$$

$$\alpha\beta' + \beta\alpha' = 0. \qquad (3)$$

66. Let us suppose that

$$\alpha = x\,i + y\,j + z\,k,$$

$$\beta = x_, i + y_, j + z_, k \quad \text{(Art. 14)}.$$

their respective conjugates will be represented by

$$\alpha' = x\,i' + y\,j' + z\,k',$$

$$\beta' = x_, i' + y_, j' + z_, k'.$$

But it is easy to see that

$$i' = i,\ j' = -j,\ k' = -k;$$

therefore we can write

$$\alpha' = x\,i - y\,j - z\,k,$$

$$\beta' = x_, i - y_, j - z_, k;$$

consequently

$$\alpha\beta' + \beta\alpha' = (x\,i + y\,j + z\,k)\,(x_, i - y_, j - z_, k)$$

$$+ (x_, i + y_, j + z_, k)\,(x\,i - y\,j - z\,k)$$

$$= 2(x\,x_, + y\,y_, + z\,z_,)\,.\,i \quad \text{(Arts. 47, 48)}, \qquad (4)$$

a third expression for $\alpha\beta' + \beta\alpha'$, which is not less important than the two preceding ones.

67. Examples.

Ex. 1. The sum of the squares of the diagonals of a parallelogram is equal to the sum of the squares of the sides.

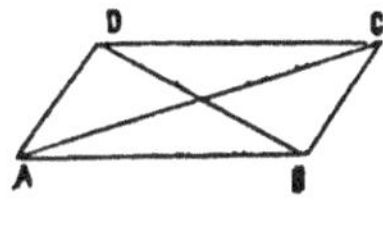

Let the side $AB = \alpha$, the side $AD = \beta$, then (Arts. 15, 16)

$$AC = \alpha + \beta.$$

$$DB = \alpha - \beta;$$

and (Art. 61)

$$(AC)' = \alpha' + \beta'.$$

$$(DB)' = \alpha' - \beta'.$$

Then

$$AC \times (AC)' = (\alpha + \beta)\,(\alpha' + \beta') = \alpha\alpha' + \beta\beta' + \alpha\beta' + \beta\alpha',$$

$$DB \times (DB)' = (\alpha - \beta)\,(\alpha' - \beta') = \alpha\alpha' + \beta\beta' - \alpha\beta' - \beta\alpha';$$

$$\therefore\quad AC \times (AC)' + DB \times (DB)' = 2\alpha\alpha' + 2\beta\beta'.$$

But (Art. 64)

$$AC \times (AC)' = (\underline{AC})^2.\,i,\quad DB \times (DB)' = (\underline{DB})^2.\,i,$$

$$\alpha\alpha' = \underline{\alpha}^2\,i = (\underline{AB})^2.\,i \quad \text{and} \quad \beta\beta' = \underline{\beta}^2\,i = (\underline{AD})^2.\,i;$$

$$(\underline{A\,C})^2\, i + (\underline{D\,B})^2\, i = 2\,(\underline{A\,B})^2\, i + 2\,(\underline{A\,D})^2\, i,$$

or

$$(\underline{A\,C})^2 + (\underline{D\,B})^2 = 2\,(\underline{A\,B})^2 + (\underline{A\,D})^2.$$

This and some of the following examples are very readily solved in the ordinary way; we give them here for illustration solely.

Ex. 2. To find the diagonal of a parallelopiped in terms of the three edges it meets, and their inclinations to one another.

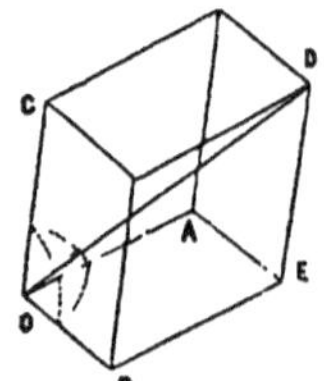

Let the edges be $O\,A = \alpha$, $O\,B = \beta$, $O\,C = \gamma$; let the inclinations be $B\,O\,C = \theta$, $C\,O\,A = \varphi$, $A\,O\,B = \Phi$. Let $O\,D = \delta$ be the diagonal required.

Then
$$O\,D = O\,B + B\,E + E\,D$$

or
$$\delta = \beta + \alpha + \gamma$$

and
$$\delta' = \beta' + \alpha' + \gamma' \quad \text{(Art. 61)}.$$

Then by multiplication.

$$\delta\delta' = \beta\beta' + \alpha\alpha' + \gamma\gamma' + (\beta\alpha' + \alpha\beta') + (\beta\gamma' + \gamma\beta') + (\alpha\gamma' + \gamma\alpha').$$

But (Art. 65)

$$\beta\alpha' + \alpha\beta' = 2\alpha\beta \,.\, \text{Cos } \Phi \,.\, i,$$

$$\beta\gamma' + \gamma\beta' = 2\underline{\beta\gamma} \,.\, \text{Cos } \theta \,.\, i,$$

$$\alpha\gamma' + \gamma\alpha' = 2\underline{\alpha\gamma}.\, \text{Cos } \varphi \,.\, i,$$

$$\delta\delta' = \underline{\delta}^2 \,.\, i, \quad \beta\beta' = \underline{\beta}^2 \,.\, i, \quad \alpha\alpha' = \underline{\alpha}^2 \,.\, i, \quad \gamma\gamma' = \underline{\gamma}^2 \,.\, i$$

$$\underline{\delta}^2 = \underline{\beta}^2 + \underline{\alpha}^2 + \underline{\gamma}^2 + 2\underline{\alpha\beta}\,.\,\text{Cos } \Phi + 2\underline{\beta\gamma}\,.\,\text{Cos } \theta + 2\underline{\alpha\gamma}\,.\,\text{Cos } \varphi.$$

Having the same terms given, we can in the same manner find the other three diagonals which pass through C, B, A; and see that, the sum of the squares of the four diagonals

$$= 4\,(\underline{\alpha}^2 + \underline{\beta}^2 + \underline{\gamma}^2).$$

Ex. 3. If O be any point whatever either in the plane of the triangle $A\,B\,C$ or out of that plane, the sum of the squares of the sides of the triangle falls short of three times the sum of the squares of the distances of the angular points from O, by the square of three times the distance of the mean point from O.

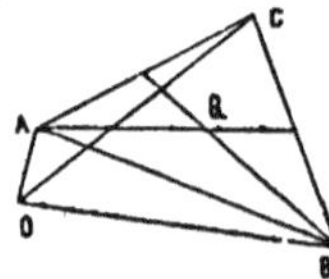

Let $O\,A = \alpha, O\,B = \beta, O\,C = \gamma$, and let G be the mean point of the triangle $A\,B\,C$, and $O\,G = \delta$.
We will first show that.

$$\delta = \tfrac{1}{3}\,(\alpha + \beta + \gamma).$$

For
$$\delta = OB + BD + DG = OB + \tfrac{1}{3} BC + \tfrac{2}{3} DA,$$

and
$$\delta = OA + AG = OA - \tfrac{1}{3} DA,$$

and
$$\delta = OC + CD + DG = OC - \tfrac{1}{3} BC + \tfrac{2}{3} DA.$$

Adding therefore these equalities,
$$3\delta = OB + OA + OC,$$

or
$$\delta = \tfrac{1}{3}(\alpha + \beta + \gamma).$$

Therefore
$$3\delta = \alpha + \beta + \gamma,$$

and
$$3\delta' = \alpha' + \beta' + \gamma';$$

and by multiplication
$$3^2 \delta\delta' = \alpha\alpha' + \beta\beta' + \gamma\gamma' + (\alpha\beta' + \beta\alpha') + (\alpha\gamma' + \gamma\alpha') + (\beta\gamma' + \gamma\beta').$$

But (Art. 65)
$$\alpha\beta' + \beta\alpha' = (\underline{\alpha}^2 + \underline{\beta}^2 - \underline{AB}^2)\,.\,i,$$

$$\alpha\gamma' + \gamma\alpha' = (\underline{\alpha}^2 + \underline{\gamma}^2 - \underline{AC}^2)\,.\,i,$$

$$\beta\gamma' + \gamma\beta' = (\underline{\beta}^2 + \underline{\gamma}^2 - \underline{BC}^2)\,.\,i;$$

and
$$\delta\delta' = \underline{\delta}^2\,.\,i,\ \ \alpha\alpha' = \underline{\alpha}^2\,.\,i,\ \ \beta\beta' = \underline{\beta}^2\,.\,i,\ \ \gamma\gamma' = \underline{\gamma}^2\,.\,i;$$

consequently
$$3\underline{\delta}^2 = 3\underline{\alpha}^2 + 3\underline{\beta}^2 + 3\underline{\gamma}^2 - (\underline{AB}^2 + \underline{AC}^2 + \underline{BC}^2),$$

or
$$\underline{AB}^2 + \underline{AC}^2 + \underline{BC}^2 = 3(\underline{\alpha}^2 + \underline{\beta}^2 + \underline{\gamma}^2) - (3\underline{\delta})^2.$$

Ex. 4. $OABCD$ being a regular pentagon, to find the algebraic expression of the side AB.

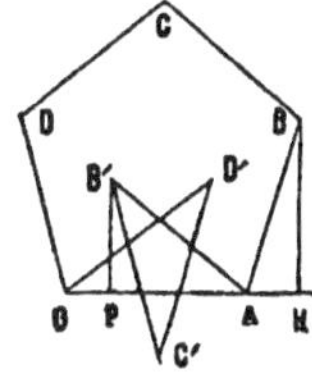

It is obvious that the angles which the directions of the sides BC, CD, DO make with the direction OH which we assume is the *principal direction* are respectively twice, three times, four times greater than the angle BAH which the side AB makes with the direction OH. Therefore if the unit of AB is x, that of BC, CD, DO will be respectively x^2, x^3, x^4 (Art. 41), and if the length of OA is represented by a, and its unit by i, then,

$$OA = ai,\ AB = ax,\ BC = ax^2,\ CD = ax^3,\ \text{and}\ DO = ax^4.$$

Besides,
$$OA + AB + BC + CD + DO = o.$$

Consequently
$$ai + ax + ax^2 + ax^3 + ax^4 = o,$$

or
$$x^4 + x^3 + x^2 + x + i = o.$$

From this equation we obtain

$$x^4 + x^3 + 2x^2 + x + i = x^2,$$

and by adding $\frac{x^2}{4}$

$$x^4 + x^3 + 2x^2 + \frac{x^2}{4} + x + i = \tfrac{1}{4} x^2$$

or
$$x^4 + \tfrac{1}{2} x^3 + x^2 + \tfrac{1}{2} x^3 + \frac{x^2}{4} + \frac{x}{2} + x^2 + \frac{x}{2} + i = \tfrac{1}{4} x^2.$$

Which can be put in the following form:

$$x^2 \left(x^2 + \tfrac{1}{2} x + i\right) + \tfrac{1}{2} x \left(x^2 + \tfrac{1}{2} x + i\right) + i \left(x^2 + \tfrac{1}{2} x + i\right) = \tfrac{1}{4} x^2,$$

or
$$\left(x^2 + \tfrac{1}{2} x + i\right)\left(x^2 + \tfrac{1}{2} x + i\right) = \tfrac{1}{4} x^2;$$

$$\left(x^2 + \tfrac{1}{2} x + i\right)^2 = \tfrac{1}{4} x^2$$

or
$$x^2 + \tfrac{1}{2} x + i = \pm \frac{x}{2} \sqrt{5}$$

$$x^2 + \tfrac{1}{2} \left(1 \mp \sqrt{5}\right) x = -i$$

(See Arts. 44, 47, 48 and 49).

From the last form, we have

$$x = -\tfrac{1}{4}\left(1 \mp \sqrt{5}\right) i \pm \tfrac{1}{4} \sqrt{16 - \left(1 \mp \sqrt{5}\right)^2} . \sqrt{-i}.$$

This equation gives for x these four values:

$$x_1 = \tfrac{1}{4}\left(\sqrt{5} - 1\right) i + \tfrac{1}{4} \sqrt{10 + 2\sqrt{5}}\sqrt{-i},$$

$$x_2 = \tfrac{1}{4}\left(\sqrt{5} - 1\right) i - \tfrac{1}{4} \sqrt{10 + 2\sqrt{5}}\sqrt{-i},$$

$$x_3 = -\tfrac{1}{4}\left(\sqrt{5} + 1\right) i - \tfrac{1}{4} \sqrt{10 - 2\sqrt{5}}\sqrt{-i},$$

$$x_4 = -\tfrac{1}{4}\left(\sqrt{5} + 1\right) i + \tfrac{1}{4} \sqrt{10 - 2\sqrt{5}}\sqrt{-i}.$$

x_1 is the unit of the side AB. If BH is perpendicular on the principal direction OH then,

$$\underline{AH} = \tfrac{1}{4} a \left(\sqrt{5} - 1\right),$$

and
$$\underline{BH} = \tfrac{1}{4} a \sqrt{10 + 2\sqrt{5}}.$$

x_2 represents the unit of the analogous side of a pentagon which we can draw under the line OA. x_3 is the unit of the side AB, of *stellated* $OAB, C, D,$. If B, P is perpendicular on OA,

$$\underline{AP} = \tfrac{1}{4} a \left(\sqrt{5} + 1\right)$$

and
$$\underline{B,P} = \tfrac{1}{4}\, a\, \sqrt{10 - 2\sqrt{5}}\; ;$$

x_4 represents the unit of the analogous side of the stellated which we can draw under the line OA.

As the side AB, of the stellated OAB,C,D, is equal to the side BC of the pentagon $OABCD$, and as the unit of BC is the square of the unit AB, x_3 must be equal to x_1^2.

Ex. 5. To find the radii of the *circles described* in and about a triangle of which the sides, in lengths, are given.

Let in this figure

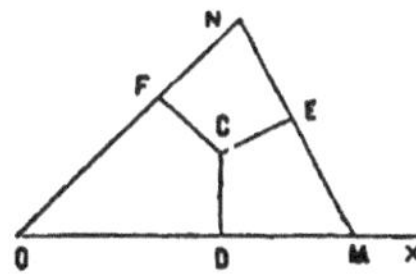

$$OD = a, \quad DM = b,$$
$$ME = b_{,}, \quad EN = c,$$
$$OF = a_{,}, \quad FN = c_{,},$$
$$DC = r, \quad EC = r_{,},$$

$CF = r_{,,}$, the angle $XMN = \varphi$, and the angle $XON = \theta$. We will suppose that DC is perpendicular on OM; EC on MN; and CF on ON. Let OX be the *principal direction*.

If α represent a unit which makes with the principal direction OX an angle of one degree (Art. 42), α^{φ} will represent the unit of MN; α^{θ} that of ON; $\alpha^{\frac{\pi}{2}}$, that of DC. $\alpha^{\frac{\pi}{2}+\varphi}$, that of FC; and $\alpha^{\frac{\pi}{2}+\theta}$, that of CF; and lastly the unit of OM will be α^0 or i. Therefore we shall have.

$$a\,i + r\,\alpha^{\frac{\pi}{2}} = a_{,}\,\alpha^{\theta} - r_{,,}\,\alpha^{\frac{\pi}{2}+\theta},$$

$$b_{,}\,\alpha^{\varphi} + r_{,}\,\alpha^{\frac{\pi}{2}+\varphi} = -\,b\,i + r\,\alpha^{\frac{\pi}{2}}, \qquad (1)$$

$$-\,c_{,}\,\alpha^{\theta} - r_{,,}\,\alpha^{\frac{\pi}{2}+\theta} = -\,c\,\alpha^{\varphi} + r_{,}\,\alpha^{\frac{\pi}{2}+\varphi}.$$

The requisite conditions to have C the centre of the *inscribed circle*, may be thus expressed,

$$a = a_{,}, \quad b = b_{,}, \quad c = c_{,}, \quad r = r_{,} = r_{,,}\;;$$

in introducing these conditions the equations will become

$$a\,i + r\,\alpha^{\frac{\pi}{2}} = a\,\alpha^{\theta} - r\,\alpha^{\frac{\pi}{2}+\theta},$$

$$b\,\alpha^{\varphi} + r\,\alpha^{\frac{\pi}{2}+\varphi} = -\,b\,i + r\,\alpha^{\frac{\pi}{2}}, \qquad (2)$$

$$-\,c\,\alpha^{\theta} - r\,\alpha^{\frac{\pi}{2}+\theta} = -\,c\,\alpha^{\varphi} + r\,\alpha^{\frac{\pi}{2}+\varphi}.$$

In multiplying these three equalities, side by side, we shall have

$$- abc\, \alpha^{\varphi+\theta} - cr^2\, \alpha^{\pi+\varphi+\theta} - br^2\, \alpha^{\pi+\theta+\varphi} - ar^2\, \alpha^{\pi+\theta+\varphi}$$

$$= abc\, \alpha^{\varphi+\theta} + cr^2\, \alpha^{\pi+\varphi+\theta} + br^2\, \alpha^{\pi+\varphi+\theta} + ar^2\, \alpha^{\pi+\theta+\varphi}.$$

As (Art. 43)
$$\alpha^{\pi+\varphi+\theta} = \alpha^{\pi}.\, \alpha^{\varphi+\theta},$$

and
$$\alpha^{\pi} = -i \text{ therefore } \alpha^{\pi+\varphi+\theta} = -\alpha^{\varphi+\theta}; \quad \text{thus}$$

$$- abc\, \alpha^{\varphi+\theta} + cr^2\, \alpha^{\varphi+\theta} + br^2\, \alpha^{\varphi+\theta} + ar^2\, \alpha^{\varphi+\theta}$$

$$= abc\, \alpha^{\varphi+\theta} - cr^2\, \alpha^{\varphi+\theta} - br^2\, \alpha^{\varphi+\theta} - ar^2\, \alpha^{\varphi+\theta},$$

and by transposing

$$2\, r^2\, (a+b+c)\, \alpha^{\varphi+\theta} - 2\, abc\, \alpha^{\varphi+\theta} = 0,$$

or

$$\left\{\, r^2\, (a+b+c) - abc\, \right\} \alpha^{\varphi+\theta} = 0.$$

$r^2\, (a+b+c) - abc$ represents only an abstract number, and to have the *product* of the factors $r^2\, (a+b+c) - abc$ and $\alpha^{\varphi+\theta}$ zero, it is necessary that one at least of these factors should also be so; but as $\alpha^{\varphi+\theta}$ cannot by supposition be zero, then

$$r^2\, (a+b+c) - abc = 0,$$

or

$$r^2 = \frac{abc}{a+b+c}.$$

Besides if we put,

$$a+b = A, \ b+c = B, \ a+c = C,$$

we shall have

$$a = \frac{A+C-B}{2}, \quad b = \frac{A+B-C}{2}, \quad c = \frac{B+C-A}{2};$$

and again if we make,

$$A+B+C = 2\, S,$$

we shall have

$$A+C-B = 2\, (S-B),$$

$$A+B-C = 2\, (S-C),$$

$$B+C-A = 2\, (S-A),$$

therefore

$$r^2 = \frac{(S-A)\,(S-B)\,(S-C)}{S};$$

$$r = \sqrt{\frac{(S-A)\,(S-B)\,(S-C)}{S}}. \qquad (3)$$

The area of the triangle O M N evidently

$$= r\,S.$$
$$= \sqrt{\{\,S\,(S-A)\,(S-B)\,(S-C)\,\}}. \qquad (4)$$

Again the area of the triangle

$$O\,M\,N = \tfrac{1}{2}\,A\,.\,C\,\operatorname{Sin}\theta = \triangle;$$

$$\operatorname{Sin}\theta = \frac{2\,\triangle}{A.C},$$

or

$$\operatorname{Sin}\theta = \frac{2}{A.C}\sqrt{\{\,S\,(S-A)\,(S-B)\,(S-C)\,\}}. \qquad (5)$$

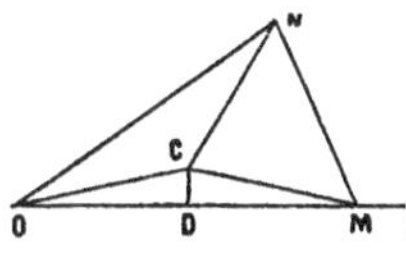

If C is the centre of the *Circumscribed Circle* and C D perpendicular on O M, the angle D C O will be equal to the angle O N M. Relying on this fact, and employing the Formula (5) the radius of the circle passing through O, M, N, is readily found. Here we shall find this radius without the aid of Formula (5).

Let $O M = A$, $M N = B$, $O N = C$, $O C = r$, the angle $M N O = \Phi$ and the angle $M O N = \theta$. Then $M C$ and $C N = r$, the angle $D O C = \tfrac{\pi}{2} - \Phi$, the angle $X M C = \pi - (\tfrac{\pi}{2} - \Phi) = \tfrac{\pi}{2} + \Phi$, and lastly the angle $X M N = (\Phi + \theta)$. Thus if we designate by α a unit which makes an angle of one degree with the principal direction, and if we take O X as the principal direction, we shall readily see that,

$$O C = r\,\alpha^{\tfrac{\pi}{2} - \Phi}, \quad M C = r\,\alpha^{\tfrac{\pi}{2} + \Phi}, \quad O N = C\,\alpha^{0},$$

$$M N = B\,\alpha^{\Phi + \theta}, \quad \text{and finally } OM = A\,\alpha^{0} = A\,i.$$

Then

$$A\,i = r\,\alpha^{\tfrac{\pi}{2} - \Phi} - \alpha^{\tfrac{\pi}{2} + \Phi};$$

and if we multiply this equality by

$$A\,i = r\,\alpha^{2\pi - \tfrac{\pi}{2} + \Phi} - r\,\alpha^{2\pi - \tfrac{\pi}{2} - \Phi} \quad (\text{Art. } 61),$$

we shall have (Art. 48)

$$A^2\,i = r^2\,\alpha^{2\pi} - r^2\,\alpha^{2\pi + 2\Phi} - r^2\,\alpha^{2\pi - 2\Phi} + r^2\,\alpha^{2\pi},$$

or as
$$\alpha^{2\pi}=i,$$

$$A^2 i = 2r^2 i - r^2\left(\alpha^{2\pi+2\Phi}+\alpha^{2\pi-2\Phi}\right)$$

or
$$\frac{2r^2 i - A^2 i}{r^2}=\alpha^{2\pi+2\Phi}+\alpha^{2\pi-2\Phi}; \qquad (a)$$

again
$$A\,i = C\,\alpha^{0}-B\,\alpha^{\Phi+0},$$

$$A\,i = C\,\alpha^{2\pi-\theta}-B\,\alpha^{2\pi-\Phi-\theta};$$

by multiplication
$$A^2 i = C^2\,\alpha^{2\pi}-BC\,\alpha^{2\pi+\Phi}-CB\,\alpha^{2\pi-\Phi}+B^2\,\alpha^{2\pi},$$

or
$$\frac{A^2-B^2-C^2}{B\,.\,C}\,i = \alpha^{2\pi+\Phi}+\alpha^{2\pi-\Phi},$$

or by squaring,
$$\frac{(A^2-B^2-C^2)^2}{B^2\,.\,C^2}\,i = \alpha^{4\pi+2\Phi}+\alpha^{4\pi-2\Phi}+2\alpha^{4\pi};$$

and as
$$\alpha^{4\pi}=i \quad\text{and}\quad \alpha^{4\pi}=\alpha^{2\pi}, \quad\text{then}$$

$$\frac{(A^2-B^2-C^2)^2}{B^2\,.\,C^2}\,i = \alpha^{2\pi+2\Phi}+\alpha^{2\pi-2\Phi}+2i,$$

hence
$$\frac{(A^2-B^2-C^2)^2-2B^2\,.\,C^2}{B^2\,.\,C^2}\,i = \alpha^{2\pi+2\Phi}+\alpha^{2\pi-2\Phi}. \qquad (b)$$

Then of the equalities (a) and (b) we have
$$\frac{(A^2-B^2-C^2)^2-2B^2\,.\,C^2}{B^2\,.\,C^2}=\frac{2r^2-A^2}{r^2},$$

and consequently
$$r^2\left\{4B^2\,.\,C^2-(A^2-B^2-C^2)^2\right\}=A^2\,.\,B^2\,.\,C^2;$$

$$r^2=\frac{A^2\,.\,B^2\,.\,C^2}{4\,B^2\,.\,C^2-(A^2-B^2-C^2)^2}.$$

Besides
$$4B^2\,.\,C^2-(A^2-B^2-C^2)^2=(2BC+A^2-B^2-C^2)(2BC-A^2+B^2+C^2)$$

$$=\left\{A^2-(B^2-2BC+C^2)\right\}\left\{(B^2+2BC+C^2)-A^2\right\}$$

$$=\left\{A^2-(B-C)^2\right\}\left\{(B+C)^2-A^2\right\}$$

$$=(A+B-C)(A-B+C)(B+C+A)(B+C-A).$$

Now if we make $A + B + C = 2S$, we shall have

$$r^2 = \frac{A^2 . B^2 . C^2}{16\,S\,(S-A)\,(S-B)\,(S-C)} ;$$

or

$$r = \frac{A . B . C}{4 \sqrt{|\,S\,(S-A)\,(S-B)\,(S-C)\,|}} . \qquad (6)$$

Ex. 6. In any quadrilateral prism, the sum of the squares of the edges exceeds the sum of the squares of the diagonals by eight times the square of the straight line which joins the points of intersection of the two pairs of diagonals.

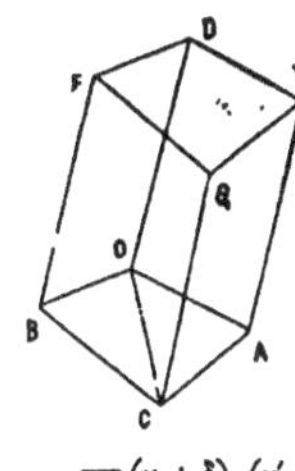

Let $OA = \alpha$, $OB = \beta$, $OC = \gamma$, $OD = \delta$; the sum of the squares of the lengths of the edges (Art. 64)

$$= 2\,|\,\alpha\alpha' + \beta\beta' + (\gamma - \alpha)\,(\gamma' - \alpha') + (\gamma - \beta)\,(\gamma' - \beta') + 2\delta\delta'\,| ,$$

$$= 2\,|\,2\alpha\alpha' + 2\beta\beta' + 2\gamma\gamma' + 2\delta\delta' - (\alpha\gamma' + \gamma\alpha') - (\gamma\beta' + \beta\gamma')\,| .$$

The sum of the squares of the lengths of the diagonals (Art. 64),

$$= (\gamma + \delta)\,(\gamma' + \delta') + (\delta - \gamma)\,(\delta' - \gamma') + (\delta + \alpha - \beta)\,(\delta' + \alpha' - \beta') + (\delta + \beta - \alpha)\,(\delta' + \beta' - \alpha')$$

$$= 2\,|\,\alpha\alpha' + \beta\beta' + \gamma\gamma' + 2\delta\delta' - (\alpha\beta' + \beta\alpha')\,| .$$

Also

$$\tfrac{1}{2}OG = \tfrac{1}{2}\,(\delta + \gamma) =$$

the distance from O to the point of bisection of CD, and therefore to the point of intersection of OG, CD; and the distance from O to the point of bisection of AF, as likewise to that of BE, and therefore to the intersection of AF, BE

$$= \frac{\beta - \alpha + \delta}{2} + \alpha = \tfrac{1}{2}\,(\delta + \alpha + \beta) ,$$

hence the straight line which joins the first point of intersection with the second

$$= \tfrac{1}{2}\,(\alpha + \beta - \gamma) ;$$

eight times the square of the length of this line (Art. 64)

$$= 2\,(\alpha + \beta - \gamma)\,(\alpha' + \beta' - \gamma')$$

$$= 2\,|\,\alpha\alpha' + \beta\beta' + \gamma\gamma' + (\alpha\beta' + \beta\alpha') - (\alpha\gamma' + \gamma\alpha') - (\beta\gamma' + \gamma\beta')\,| ,$$

which, added to the sum of the squares of the lengths of the diagonals makes up the sum of the squares of the lenghts of the edges.

68. We have seen that x, y and z being *rectangular coordinates* (Art. 14) $\rho = xi + yj + zk$; If in this expression we make $yj + zk = \eta$, we shall have $\rho = xi + \eta$. It is obvious that this η, being on the plane passing through the direction OX and through ρ, is perpendicular to the principal direction OX. Therefore let us represent the lines α, β in this manner, and

Let

$$\alpha = x\,i + \eta,$$

$$\beta = x,\,i + \eta,.$$

and their conjugates

$$\alpha' = x\,i + \acute\eta,$$

$$\beta' = x,\,i + \acute\eta,.$$

Thus

$$\alpha\beta' = x\,x,\,i + x,\,\acute\eta + x\,\acute\eta, + \eta\,\acute\eta, \quad \text{(Art. 47)},$$

$$\beta\alpha' = x,\,x\,i + x\,\eta, + x,\,\acute\eta + \eta,\,\acute\eta,$$

and by addition

$$\alpha\beta' + \beta\alpha' = 2x\,x,\,i + x,\,(\eta + \acute\eta) + x(\eta, + \acute\eta,) + (\eta\,\acute\eta, + \eta,\,\acute\eta);$$

but, $\eta + \acute\eta = 0$, and $\eta, + \acute\eta, = 0$, and besides if Φ represent the angle which is between η and η, transposed to the same origin,

$$\eta\,\acute\eta, + \eta,\,\acute\eta = 2\,\underline{\eta\,\eta},\ \text{Cos}\ \Phi\,.\,\dot{i}\quad \text{(Art. 65).}\quad \text{Therefore}$$

$$\alpha\beta' + \beta\alpha' = 2x\,x,\,i + 2\,\underline{\eta\,\eta},\ \text{Cos}\ \Phi\,.\,i.$$

Example. To find the cosine of an angle of a spherical triangle in terms of the cosines and sines of the sides.

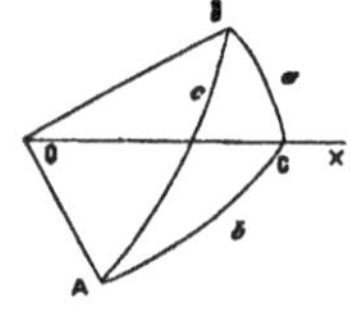

Let us assume that α and β in the last Formula are two units, and that in this figure α represents O A; and β, O B. Then necessarily

$$x = \text{Cos}\ b,\ x, = \text{Cos}\ a,\ \underline\eta = \text{Sin}\ b,\ \underline\eta, = \text{Sin a},\ \Phi = \text{angle A C B},$$

and

$$\alpha\beta' + \beta\alpha' = 2\,\text{Cos}\ c\,.\,i\ \text{(Art. 65)}$$

Thus

$$2\,\text{Cos}\ c\,.\,i = 2\,\text{Cos}\ a\,.\,\text{Cos}\ b\,.\,i + 2\,\text{Sin}\ a\,.\,\text{Sin}\ b\,.\,\text{Cos C}\,.\,i,$$

or

$$\text{Cos}\ c = \text{Cos}\ a\,.\,\text{Cos}\ b + \text{Sin}\ a\,.\,\text{Sin}\ b\,.\,\text{Cos C}.$$

CHAPTER III.

SPECIAL PERPENDICULAR.

69. Let us suppose that α represents a line OA; β, a line O B; and that $\overline{\text{O A}} = a$, $\text{O B} = b$. A perpendicular erected on the plane which passes through the lines $\overline{\alpha,\,\beta}$, and having a length equal to $a\,.\,b$. Sin A O B performs a very important part in the calculations of Linear Algebra; we shall call it the *Special Perpendicular* of these two lines α and β. It is scarcely necessary to say that this number ab Sin A O B is equal to the area of the parallelogram which has O A and O B as two adjacent sides.

70. The special perpendicular of α and β will be considered as having such a direction that in placing ourselves at the opening of the angle which is between O A and OB,

in such a manner that O B or β may be at our right and O A or α at our left, and on regarding the point O, we shall see agreeably to our ordinary conceptions that this perpendicular is raised on the plane A O B; if we suppose ourselves placed in the opening of the angle A O B in such a manner that α will be at our right and β at our left the Special perpendicular which we should have conceived as rising on the plane B O A, will be that of β and α.

71. We will represent the special perpendicular of α, β by $\prod_{\alpha\beta}$ or $\Pi_{\alpha\beta}$, and that of β, α by $\prod_{\beta\alpha}$ or $\Pi_{\beta\alpha}$; it is evident that

$$\prod_{\alpha\beta} = -\prod_{\beta\alpha}, \quad \text{or} \quad \prod_{\alpha\beta} + \prod_{\beta\alpha} = 0.$$

It follows from the very definition of the special perpendicular that the absolute number or length of $\prod_{\alpha\beta}$ is $a\,b\,\operatorname{Sin}\theta$, θ being the angle which is between α, β transferred to the same origin. It is evident that a, being an abstract number, the special perpendicular of $a\,\alpha$ and β, or $\prod_{a\,\alpha\,\beta}$ will be $= a\,\prod_{\alpha\beta}$; the special perpendicular of $-\alpha$ and β is $-\prod_{\alpha\beta}$, that of α, $-\beta$ is also $-\prod_{\alpha\beta}$; that of $-\alpha$, $-\beta$, is $\prod_{\alpha\beta}$. If $\alpha = \beta$, and x an abstract number, the special perpendicular of $x\,\alpha$ and β, or that of α and $x\,\beta$ wille be $= o$;

or

$$\prod_{x\,\alpha\,\alpha} = o, \quad \prod_{\alpha\,x\,\alpha} = o.$$

72. If α and β are given, we shall be able to determine $\prod_{\alpha\beta}$, and consequently $\prod_{\beta\alpha}$. Let us first find the absolute length of $\prod_{\alpha\beta}$. If we represent by θ the angle which is between α and β, transferred to a common origin, we shall have

$$\alpha\beta' + \beta\alpha' = 2\,a\,b\,\operatorname{Cos}\theta.\,i \quad \text{(Art. 65)}.$$

From this

$$\alpha\beta' + \beta\alpha' = 2\,a\,b\,\sqrt{1 - \operatorname{Sin}^2\theta}\;i,$$

or

$$(\alpha\beta' + \beta\alpha')^2 = 4\,a^2\,b^2\,(1 - \operatorname{Sin}^2\theta).\,i \quad \text{(Art. 48)},$$

$$a\,b\,\operatorname{Sin}\theta.\,i = \tfrac{1}{2}\sqrt{\left\{4\,a^2\,b^2\,i - (\alpha\beta' + \beta\alpha')^2\right\}}$$

which gives according to the very definition the absolute length of $\prod_{\alpha\beta}$ or that of $\prod_{\beta\alpha}$, in terms of α and β. Now, let us try to find the unit of the special perpendicular $\prod_{\alpha\beta}$, we will represent it by u, and assuming that α and β are given we will write them also in this form

$$\alpha = x_1\,i + y_1\,j + z_1\,k \quad \text{(Art. 14)},$$
$$\beta = x_2\,i + y_2\,j + z_2\,k,$$

and also

$$u = x_3\,i + y_3\,j + z_3\,k.$$

The direction of u being perpendicular to the lines α and β, we must have (Art. 65)

$$\alpha u' + u \alpha' = 0,$$

$$\beta u' + u \beta' = 0;$$

on replacing in these two linear equations α, α', β, β', , u, u' by their equivalents, we shall have these two numerical equations (Art. 66)

$$x_1 x_3 + y_1 y_3 + z_1 z_3 = 0, \tag{1}$$

$$x_2 x_3 + y_2 y_3 + z_2 z_3 = 0; \tag{2}$$

and as u is but a linear unit, we have $u . u' = i$ (At. 64), or

$$x_3^2 + y_3^2 + z_3^2 = 1. \tag{3}$$

Of these three numerical equations, we shall find,

$$x_3 = \frac{z_1 y_2 - y_1 z_2}{y_1 x_2 - x_1 y_2}\, z_3,$$

$$y_3 = \frac{x_1 z_2 - z_1 x_2}{y_1 x_2 - x_1 y_2}\, z_3,$$

$$z_3 = \pm \frac{y_1 x_2 - x_1 y_2}{\sqrt{\left\{ (z_1 y_2 - y_1 z_2)^2 + (x_1 z_2 - z_1 x_2)^2 + (y_1 x_2 - x_1 y_2)^2 \right\}}}.$$

Thus the equation $u = x_3 i + y_3 j + z_3 k$ will become

$$u = \frac{z_1 y_2 - y_1 z_2}{y_1 x_2 - x_1 y_2}\, z_3 i + \frac{x_1 z_2 - z_1 x_2}{y_1 x_2 - x_1 y_2}\, z_3 j + z_3 k.$$

Therefore by multiplying this unit u by $a b \operatorname{Sin} \theta$, we shall have $\displaystyle\prod_{\alpha \beta}$.

73. We have already found that

$$a b \operatorname{Sin} \theta . i = \tfrac{1}{2} \sqrt{\left\{ 4 a^2 b^2 i - (\alpha \beta' + \beta \alpha')^2 \right\}},$$

or $\qquad a b \operatorname{Sin} \theta\, i = \tfrac{1}{2} \sqrt{\left\{ 4 \alpha \alpha' . \beta \beta' - (\alpha \beta' + \beta \alpha')^2 \right\}}$ (Arts. 48, 64);

if now we put into this equation the equivalents of α, α', β and β' we shall have,

$$a b \operatorname{Sin} \theta = \sqrt{\left\{ (x_1 y_2 - y_1 z_2)^2 + (x_1 z_2 - z_1 x_2)^2 + (y_1 x_2 - x_1 y_2)^2 \right\}}.$$

Then $a b \operatorname{Sin} \theta . u$, or

$$\prod_{\alpha \beta} = (x_1 y_2 - y_1 z_2) i + (x_1 z_2 - z_1 x_2) j + (y_1 x_2 - x_1 y_2) k,$$

which is the special perpendicular of α and β; also,

$$\prod_{\beta \alpha} = (y_1 z_2 - z_1 y_2) i + (z_1 x_2 - x_1 z_2) j + (x_1 y_2 - y_1 x_2) k.$$

74. In a pyramid $CAOB$ let $OA = \alpha$, $OB = \beta$ and $OC = \gamma$. We know that, if the hight CD of the pyramid $COAB$ is H, three times the volume of this pyramid will $= H \times$ the area of the triangle AOB; and if the angle $AOB = \theta$, the area of the triangle $AOB = \frac{1}{2}\underline{\alpha\,\beta}$. Sin θ. Therefore if V represents the volume of this pyramid, we have

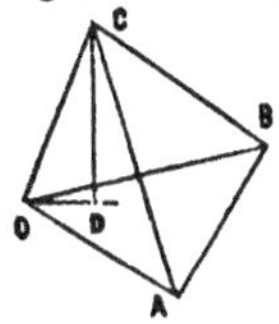

$$6\,V = \underline{\alpha\,\beta}\ \text{Sin } \theta \times H\,;$$

and if the angle $DOC = \varphi$, then $H = \underline{\gamma}$ Sin φ;

consequently

$$6\,V = \underline{\alpha\,\beta\,\gamma}\ \text{Sin } \theta.\ \text{Sin } \varphi\ .$$

But according to Art. 65

$$\gamma \prod_{\alpha\beta}' + \prod_{\alpha\beta} \gamma' = 2\underline{\gamma}\ .\ N\left(\prod_{\alpha\beta}\right) \text{Cos } (\tfrac{\pi}{2}-\varphi).\,i\ \text{(Art. 4)},$$

and as

$$N\left(\prod_{\alpha\beta}\right) = 2\,\underline{\alpha\,\beta}\ \text{Sin } \theta\ \text{(Art. 69)},$$

then

$$\gamma \prod_{\alpha\beta}' + \prod_{\alpha\beta} \gamma' = 2\,\underline{\alpha\,\beta\,\gamma}\ \text{Sin } \theta.\ \text{Sin } \varphi\ .\,i,$$

$$\gamma \prod_{\alpha\beta}' + \prod_{\alpha\beta} \gamma' = 12\ V\ .\,i.$$

In the same manner we can also find that

$$\beta \prod_{\gamma\alpha}' + \prod_{\gamma\alpha} \beta' = 12\ V\ .\,i,$$

$$\alpha \prod_{\beta\gamma}' + \prod_{\beta\gamma} \alpha' = 12\ V\ .\,i.$$

75. From this comes the following important theorem. When three lines represented respectively by α, β, γ are not in the same plane, we have

$$\gamma \prod_{\alpha\beta}' + \prod_{\alpha\beta} \gamma' = \beta \prod_{\gamma\alpha}' + \prod_{\gamma\alpha} \beta' = \alpha \prod_{\beta\gamma}' + \prod_{\beta\gamma} \alpha'.$$

From the inspection of this formula we shall see by what law α, β and γ there change their places on quitting the bottom of $\prod$ to range themselves by its side, or *vice versâ*. It is very necessary to remark that in this formula we assume that in placing ourselves between α, β leaving β to our right and α to our left, and in regarding the point O, we shall see γ above the plane passing through α, β. Also, if we place ourselves between γ, α, or between β, γ, leaving α or γ at our right and γ or β to our left and in regarding the point O, we shall see β above the plane which passes through γ, α; and α above the plane which passes through β, γ.

76. If α, β, γ are on the same plane, $\varphi = 0$;

therefore
$$2 \underline{\alpha\,\beta\,\gamma}\ \mathrm{Sin}\ \theta \,.\, \mathrm{Sin}\ \varphi = 0,$$

and
$$\gamma \prod_{\alpha\beta}' + \prod_{\alpha\beta} \gamma' = \beta \prod_{\gamma\alpha}' + \prod_{\gamma\alpha} \beta' = \alpha \prod_{\beta\gamma}' + \prod_{\beta\gamma} \alpha' = 0.$$

Conversely, if $\gamma \prod_{\alpha\beta}' + \prod_{\alpha\beta} \gamma' = 0$, none of the lines α, β, γ being themselves 0, we must have either $\theta = 0$ or $\varphi = 0$; hence in either case the three lines are coplanar.

77. Since $\prod_{\alpha\beta}$ is perpendicular to the plane $A\,O\,B$ (Fig. of Art. 74) and $\prod_{\beta\gamma}$ is perpendicular to the plane $B\,O\,C$ $\prod_{\alpha\beta}$, $\prod_{\beta\gamma}$ are both perpendicular to $O\,B$ the line along which is β; $O\,B$ is perpendicular to the plane which passes through $\prod_{\alpha\beta}$, $\prod_{\beta\gamma}$, and therefore is in the direction of

$$\prod_{\underset{\alpha\beta\ \beta\gamma}{\Pi\ \Pi}}\ ; \quad \text{hence, } m \text{ being a number}, \qquad \prod_{\underset{\alpha\beta\ \beta\gamma}{\Pi\ \Pi}} = m\,\beta.$$

If $O\,A = \alpha$, $O\,B = \beta$, $O\,D = \delta$, $O\,E = \epsilon$; and if the planes $A\,O\,B$, $D\,O\,E$ intersect in $O\,P$; it follows as seen above, that, $\prod_{\alpha\beta}$ and $\prod_{\delta\epsilon}$ being both perpendicular to $O\,P$,

$$\prod_{\underset{\alpha\beta\ \delta\epsilon}{\Pi\ \Pi}}$$

is along $O\,P$ and is therefore $= n.\ O\,P$, n being a number.

78. *Formulæ*

We have already seen (Art. 65) that

$$\alpha\,\beta' + \beta\,\alpha' = \alpha'\beta + \beta'\alpha = 2\,\underline{\alpha\,\beta}\ \mathrm{Cos}\ \theta . \, i = (a^2 + b^2 - d^2)\, i, \qquad (1)$$

$$\prod_{\alpha\,\beta} = -\prod_{\beta\,\alpha} \quad (\text{Art. 71}). \qquad (2)$$

Let the angle which is between the lines α, β transferred to the same origin, be θ. Evidently we have

$$\underline{\alpha^2\,\beta^2} = \underline{\alpha^2\,\beta^2}\ \mathrm{Cos}^2\,\theta + \underline{\alpha^2\,\beta^2}\ \mathrm{Sin}^2\,\theta ;$$

but
$$\underline{\alpha^2\,\beta^2}\ \mathrm{Cos}^2\,\theta = \tfrac{1}{4}\,(\underline{\alpha\,\beta' + \beta\,\alpha'})^2 \qquad (\text{Art. 4}),$$

and
$$\underline{\alpha^2\,\beta^2}\ \mathrm{Sin}^2\,\theta = N^2 \Big(\prod_{\alpha\,\beta}\Big) \qquad (\text{Art. 4});$$

hence
$$\underline{\alpha^2\,\beta^2} = \tfrac{1}{4}\,(\underline{\alpha\,\beta' + \beta\,\alpha'})^2 + N^2\Big(\prod_{\alpha\,\beta}\Big). \qquad (3)$$

Let
$$\alpha = \gamma + \delta, \quad \beta = \rho + \omega.$$

From these we can deduce the following numerical equation

$$\underline{\alpha\,\beta' + \beta\,\alpha'} = \underline{\gamma\,\rho'} + \underline{\rho\,\gamma'} + \underline{\delta\,\rho'} + \underline{\rho\,\delta'} + \underline{\gamma\,\omega'} + \underline{\omega\,\gamma'} + \underline{\delta\,\omega'} + \underline{\omega\,\delta'} ; \qquad (4)$$

for we have

$$\alpha\beta' = (\gamma+\delta)(\rho'+\omega') = \gamma\rho' + \delta\rho' + \gamma\omega' + \delta\omega',$$

$$\beta\alpha' = (\rho+\omega)(\gamma'+\delta') = \rho\gamma' + \rho\alpha' + \omega\gamma' + \omega\delta';$$

therefore by adding these two equations one to the other, we shall have,

$$(\alpha\beta'+\beta\alpha') = (\gamma\rho'+\rho\gamma') + (\gamma\omega'+\omega\gamma') + (\delta\rho'+\rho\delta') + (\omega\delta'+\delta\omega').$$

This theorem still remains good when α and β compose more than two lines.

We know that when $\alpha=\beta$

$$\prod_{\alpha\beta} \quad \text{or} \quad \prod_{\alpha\alpha} = 0$$

and

$$(\alpha\beta'+\beta\alpha') \quad \text{or} \quad \alpha\alpha'+\alpha\alpha' = 2\,\alpha^2\,i.$$

Let
$$\alpha = x_1 i + y_1 j + z_1 k, \quad \beta = x_2 i + y_2 j + z_2 k.$$

We shall have
$$\alpha\beta'+\beta\alpha' = \alpha'\beta+\beta'\alpha = 2(x_1 x_2 + y_1 y_2 + z_1 z_2)\,i \quad \text{(Art. 66).} \quad (5)$$

or
$$\alpha\beta'-\beta\alpha' = 2(z_1 y_2 - y_1 z_2)\,i + 2(y_1 x_2 - x_1 y_2)\,j + 2(z_1 x_2 - x_1 z_2)\,k. \quad (6)$$

We have also seen already (Art. 73) that

$$\prod_{\alpha\beta} = (z_1 y_2 - y_1 z_2)\,i + (x_1 z_2 - z_1 x_2)\,j + (y_1 x_2 - x_1 y_2)\,k. \quad (7)$$

The frequency of the application of this last formula or theorem in what follows, allows me to recommend to the reader to notice particularly, and to keep constantly in mind the law according to which the terms of this Formula are formed from the terms of α and β.

If (Art. 14)
$$\alpha = x_1 i + y_1 j + z_1 k,$$
$$\beta = x_2 i + y_2 j + z_2 k,$$
$$\gamma = x_3 i + y_3 j + z_3 k,$$

and
$$\delta = x_4 i + y_4 j + z_4 k;$$

by addition we shall have
$$\alpha+\beta = (x_1 + x_2)\,i + (y_1 + y_2)\,j + (z_1 + z_2)\,k,$$

$$\gamma+\delta = (x_3 + x_4)\,i + (y_3 + y_4)\,j + (z_3 + z_4)\,k;$$

and by Formula (7)
$$\prod_{(\alpha+\beta)(\gamma+\delta)} = |\,(x_1 + x_2)(y_3 + y_4) - (y_1 + y_2)(x_3 + x_4)\,|\,i$$
$$+ |\,(x_1 + x_2)(z_3 + z_4) - (z_1 + z_2)(x_3 + x_4)\,|\,j$$
$$+ |\,(y_1 + y_2)(x_3 + x_4) - (x_1 + x_2)(y_3 + y_4)\,|\,k;$$

after having performed the multiplication and arranged the terms, we shall have

$$\prod_{(\alpha+\beta)(\gamma+\delta)} = (x_1 y_3 - y_1 z_3)\, i + (x_1 z_3 - z_1 x_3)\, j + (y_1 x_3 - x_1 y_3)\, k$$
$$+ (x_2 y_3 - y_2 z_3)\, i + (x_2 z_3 - z_2 x_3)\, j + (y_2 x_3 - x_2 y_3)\, k$$
$$+ (x_1 y_4 - y_1 z_4)\, i + (x_1 z_4 - z_1 x_4)\, j + (y_1 x_4 - x_1 y_4)\, k$$
$$+ (x_2 y_4 - y_2 z_4)\, i + (x_2 z_4 - z_2 x_4)\, j + (y_2 x_4 - x_2 y_4)\, k,$$

or again by Formula (7)

$$\prod_{(\alpha+\beta)(\gamma+\delta)} = \prod_{(\alpha+\beta)(\gamma+\delta)} = \prod_{\alpha\gamma} + \prod_{\alpha\delta} + \prod_{\beta\gamma} + \prod_{\beta\delta}. \qquad (8)$$

It is well to observe that the formation of the terms of this Formula follows the same law as the terms of a polynomial multiplication.

If α, β, γ are three lines (*not coplaner*) we shall have (Art. 75)

$$\gamma \prod_{\alpha\beta}' + \prod_{\alpha\beta} \gamma' = \beta \prod_{\gamma\alpha}' + \prod_{\gamma\alpha} \beta' = \alpha \prod_{\beta\gamma}' + \prod_{\beta\gamma} \alpha', \qquad (9)$$

and by Formula (2)

$$\gamma \prod_{\alpha\beta}' + \prod_{\alpha\beta} \gamma' = - \left(\gamma \prod_{\beta\alpha}' + \prod_{\beta\alpha} \gamma \right). \qquad (10)$$

If

$$\alpha = x_1 i + y_1 j + z_1 k, \quad \beta = x_2 i + y_2 j + z_2 k;$$

we have

$$\prod_{\alpha\beta} = (x_1 y_2 - y_1 z_2)\, i + (x_1 z_2 - z_1 x_2)\, j + (y_1 x_2 - x_1 y_2)\, k;$$

and again if

$$\gamma = x_3 i + y_3 j + z_3 k,$$

we shall have by Formula (5)

$$\gamma \prod_{\alpha\beta}' + \prod_{\alpha\beta} \gamma = 2 \left\{ x_3 (x_1 y_2 - y_1 z_2) + y_3 (x_1 z_2 - z_1 x_2) + z_3 (y_1 x_2 - x_1 y_2) \right\} i$$

$$= 2 \begin{vmatrix} x_1 & y_1 & x_1 \\ x_2 & y_2 & x_2 \\ z_3 & y_3 & x_3 \end{vmatrix} i. \qquad (11)$$

We have seen that the volume of the pyramid $O\,A\,B\,C$ (when $O\,A = \alpha$, $O\,B = \beta$, $O\,C = \gamma$) is one twelfth of the above.

If

$$\alpha = x_1 i + y_1 j + z_1 k, \quad \beta = x_2 i + y_2 j + z_2 k, \quad \gamma = x_3 i + y_3 j + z_3 k;$$

in replacing β by $\prod_{\beta\gamma}$ in Formula (7), we shall have

$$\prod_{\alpha \prod_{\beta\gamma}} = \{ z_1 (x_2 z_3 - z_2 x_3) - y_1 (y_2 x_3 - x_2 y_3) \} i$$
$$+ \{ x_1 (y_2 x_3 - x_2 y_3) - z_1 (z_2 y_3 - y_2 z_3) \} j$$

$$+ \{ y_1 (z_2 y_3 - y_3 z_3) - x_1 (x_2 z_3 - z_2 x_3) \} k$$

$$= (x_1 x_3 + y_1 y_3 + z_1 z_3) x_2 i - (x_1 x_2 + y_1 y_2 + z_1 z_2) x_3 i$$

$$+ (x_1 x_3 + y_1 y_3 + z_1 z_3) y_2 j - (x_1 x_2 + y_1 y_2 + z_1 z_2) y_3 j,$$

$$+ (x_1 x_3 + y_1 y_3 + z_1 z_3) z_2 k - (x_1 x_2 + y_1 y_2 + z_1 z_2) z_3 k$$

$$= (x_1 x_3 + y_1 y_3 + z_1 z_3)(x_2 i + y_2 j + z_2 k)$$

$$- (x_1 x_2 + y_1 y_2 + z_1 z_2)(x_3 i + y_3 j + z_3 k);$$

then by Formula (5)

$$\prod_{\substack{\alpha\,\Pi \\ \beta\,\gamma}} = \tfrac{1}{2}(\alpha\gamma' + \gamma\alpha')\,\beta - \tfrac{1}{2}(\alpha\beta' + \beta\alpha')\,\gamma. \tag{12}$$

Hence

$$\prod_{\substack{\Pi\,\alpha \\ \beta\gamma}} = \tfrac{1}{2}(\alpha\beta' + \beta\alpha')\,\gamma - \tfrac{1}{2}(\alpha\gamma' + \gamma\alpha')\,\beta. \tag{13}$$

Whether we employ Formula (12), or whether we make use of the method which gave it to us, we can have

$$\prod_{\substack{\Pi\,\gamma \\ \alpha\beta}} = \tfrac{1}{2}(\alpha\gamma' + \gamma\alpha')\,\beta - \tfrac{1}{2}(\beta\gamma' + \gamma\beta')\,\alpha. \tag{14}$$

$$\prod_{\substack{\alpha\,\Pi \\ \beta\gamma}} - \prod_{\substack{\Pi\,\gamma \\ \alpha\beta}} = \tfrac{1}{2}(\beta\gamma' + \gamma\beta')\,\alpha - \tfrac{1}{2}(\alpha\beta + \beta\alpha')\,\gamma,$$

or

$$\prod_{\substack{\alpha\,\Pi \\ \beta\gamma}} - \tfrac{1}{2}(\beta\gamma' + \gamma\beta')\,\alpha = \prod_{\substack{\Pi\,\gamma \\ \alpha\beta}} - \tfrac{1}{2}(\alpha\beta' + \beta\alpha')\,\gamma. \tag{15}$$

We have by Foamula (12)

$$\prod_{\substack{\alpha\,\Pi \\ \beta\gamma}} = \tfrac{1}{2}(\alpha\gamma' + \gamma\alpha')\,\beta - \tfrac{1}{2}(\alpha\beta' + \beta\alpha')\,\gamma,$$

$$\prod_{\substack{\beta\,\Pi \\ \gamma\alpha}} = \tfrac{1}{2}(\beta\alpha' + \alpha\beta')\,\gamma - \tfrac{1}{2}(\beta\gamma' + \gamma\beta')\,\alpha,$$

$$\prod_{\substack{\gamma\,\Pi \\ \alpha\beta}} = \tfrac{1}{2}(\gamma\beta' + \beta\gamma')\,\alpha - \tfrac{1}{2}(\gamma\alpha' + \alpha\gamma')\,\beta;$$

therefore by adding

$$\prod_{\substack{\alpha\,\Pi \\ \beta\gamma}} + \prod_{\substack{\beta\,\Pi \\ \gamma\alpha}} + \prod_{\substack{\gamma\,\Pi \\ \alpha\beta}} = 0. \tag{16}$$

By Formula 12

$$\prod_{\substack{\alpha\,\Pi \\ \beta\gamma}} = \tfrac{1}{2}(\alpha\gamma' + \gamma\alpha')\,\beta - \tfrac{1}{2}(\alpha\beta' + \beta\alpha')\,\gamma;$$

by putting here $\prod_{\alpha\beta}$ instead of α we shall have

$$\prod_{\substack{\prod \ \prod \\ \alpha\beta \ \beta\gamma}} = \tfrac{1}{2}\left(\prod_{\alpha\beta}\gamma + \gamma\prod_{\alpha\beta}'\right)\beta - \tfrac{1}{2}\left(\prod_{\alpha\beta}\beta' + \beta\prod_{\alpha\beta}'\right)\gamma;$$

but the lines $\prod_{\alpha\beta}$ and β being perpendicular the one to the other, $\prod_{\alpha\beta}\beta' + \beta\prod_{\alpha\beta}' = 0$ (Art. 65), consequently

$$\prod_{\substack{\prod \ \prod \\ \alpha\beta \ \beta\gamma}} = \tfrac{1}{2}\left(\gamma\prod_{\alpha\beta}' + \prod_{\alpha\beta}\gamma'\right)\beta = \tfrac{1}{2}\left(\alpha\prod_{\beta\gamma}' + \prod_{\beta\gamma}\alpha'\right)\beta. \qquad (17)$$

If in Formula (12) we had replaced α by $\prod_{\alpha\delta}$, we should have found,

$$\prod_{\substack{\prod \ \prod \\ \alpha\delta \ \beta\gamma}} = \tfrac{1}{2}\left(\prod_{\alpha\delta}\gamma + \gamma\prod_{\alpha\delta}'\right)\beta - \tfrac{1}{2}\left(\prod_{\alpha\delta}\beta' + \beta\prod_{\alpha\delta}'\right)\gamma. \qquad (18)$$

By this last Formula

$$\prod_{\substack{\prod \ \prod \\ \beta\gamma \ \alpha\delta}} = \tfrac{1}{2}\left(\prod_{\beta\gamma}\delta' + \delta\prod_{\beta\gamma}'\right)\alpha - \tfrac{1}{2}\left(\prod_{\beta\gamma}\alpha' + \alpha\prod_{\beta\gamma}'\right)\delta;$$

but by the Formula (2)

$$\prod_{\substack{\prod \ \prod \\ \beta\gamma \ \alpha\delta}} + \prod_{\substack{\prod \ \prod \\ \alpha\delta \ \beta\gamma}} = 0;$$

then

$$\left(\prod_{\alpha\delta}\gamma + \gamma\prod_{\alpha\delta}'\right)\beta - \left(\prod_{\alpha\delta}\beta' + \beta\prod_{\alpha\delta}'\right)\gamma + \left(\prod_{\beta\gamma}\delta' + \delta\prod_{\beta\gamma}'\right)\alpha - \left(\prod_{\beta\gamma}\alpha' + \alpha\prod_{\beta\gamma}'\right)\delta = 0;$$

but by Formulæ (9) and (10)

$$\gamma\prod_{\alpha\delta}' + \prod_{\alpha\delta}\gamma' = \delta\prod_{\gamma\alpha}' + \prod_{\gamma\alpha}\delta' = -\left(\delta\prod_{\alpha\gamma}' + \prod_{\alpha\gamma}\delta'\right),$$

$$\beta\prod_{\alpha\delta}' + \prod_{\alpha\delta}\beta' = \delta\prod_{\beta\alpha}' + \prod_{\beta\alpha}\delta = -\left(\delta\prod_{\alpha\beta}' + \prod_{\alpha\beta}\delta'\right),$$

$$\alpha\prod_{\beta\gamma}' + \prod_{\beta\gamma}\alpha' = \gamma\prod_{\alpha\beta}' + \prod_{\alpha\beta}\gamma';$$

consequently

$$\left(\delta\prod_{\beta\gamma}' + \prod_{\beta\gamma}\delta'\right)\alpha - \left(\delta\prod_{\alpha\gamma}' + \prod_{\alpha\gamma}\delta'\right)\beta + \left(\delta\prod_{\alpha\beta}' + \prod_{\alpha\beta}\delta'\right)\gamma - \left(\gamma\prod_{\alpha\beta}' + \prod_{\alpha\beta}\gamma'\right)\delta = 0;$$

$$\therefore \left(\gamma\prod_{\alpha\beta}' + \prod_{\alpha\beta}\gamma'\right)\delta = \left(\delta\prod_{\beta\gamma}' + \prod_{\beta\gamma}\delta'\right)\alpha - \left(\delta\prod_{\alpha\gamma}' + \prod_{\alpha\gamma}\delta'\right)\beta + \left(\delta\prod_{\alpha\beta}' + \prod_{\alpha\beta}\delta'\right)\gamma,$$

or $\left(\gamma\prod_{\alpha\beta}' + \prod_{\alpha\beta}\gamma'\right)\delta = \left(\delta\prod_{\beta\gamma}' + \prod_{\beta\gamma}\delta'\right)\alpha + \left(\delta\prod_{\gamma\alpha}' + \prod_{\gamma\alpha}\delta'\right)\beta + \left(\delta\prod_{\alpha\beta}' + \prod_{\alpha\beta}\delta'\right)\gamma.$ (19)

We can put the last Formula in this form

$$\delta = \frac{1}{N\left(\gamma \prod'_{\alpha\beta} + \prod_{\alpha\beta} \gamma'\right)} \left\{ \left(\delta \prod'_{\beta\gamma} + \prod_{\beta\gamma} \delta'\right) \alpha + \left(\delta \prod'_{\gamma\alpha} + \prod_{\gamma\alpha} \delta'\right) \beta + \left(\delta \prod'_{\alpha\beta} + \prod_{\alpha\beta} \delta'\right) \gamma \right\}.$$

This equation expresses a line in terms of three other lines.

Let $\quad \alpha = x_1 i + y_1 j + z_1 k, \quad \beta = x_2 i + y_2 j + z_2 k, \quad \gamma = x_3 i + y_3 j + z_3 k,$
$$\delta = x_4 i + y_4 j + z_4 k;$$

by Formula (11)

$$\delta \prod'_{\beta\gamma} + \prod_{\beta\gamma} \delta = 2 \left\{ x_4 \ (z_2 y_3 - y_2 z_3) + y_4 \ (x_2 z_3 - z_2 x_3) + z_4 \ (y_2 x_3 - x_2 y_3) \right\} i,$$

$$\delta \prod'_{\gamma\alpha} + \prod_{\gamma\alpha} \delta = 2 \left\{ x_4 \ (z_3 y_1 - y_3 z_1) + y_4 \ (x_3 z_1 - z_3 x_1) + z_4 \ (y_3 x_1 - x_3 y_1) \right\} i,$$

$$\delta \prod'_{\alpha\beta} + \prod_{\alpha\beta} \delta = 2 \left\{ x_4 \ (z_1 y_2 - y_1 z_2) + y_4 \ (x_1 z_2 - z_1 x_2) + z_4 \ (y_1 x_2 - x_1 y_2) \right\} i.$$

Now on multiplying the first of these three equalities by $\alpha = x_1 i + y_1 j + z_1 k$; the second, by $\beta = x_2 i + y_2 j + z_2 k$; the third by $\gamma = x_3 i + y_3 j + z_3 k$; and finally in adding the products we shall have

$$\left(\delta \prod'_{\beta\gamma} + \prod_{\beta\gamma} \delta'\right) \alpha + \left(\delta \prod'_{\gamma\alpha} + \prod_{\gamma\alpha} \delta'\right) \beta + \left(\delta \prod'_{\alpha\beta} + \prod_{\alpha\beta} \delta'\right) \gamma$$

which is the second member of Formula (19) and

$$= 2x_1 x_4 \ (z_2 y_3 - y_2 z_3) i + 2 y_1 y_4 \ (x_2 z_3 - z_2 x_3) j + 2 z_1 z_4 \ (y_2 x_3 - x_2 y_3) k$$
$$+ 2 x_2 x_4 \ (z_3 y_1 - y_3 z_1) i + 2 y_2 y_4 \ (x_3 z_1 - z_3 x_1) j + 2 z_2 z_4 \ (y_3 x_1 - x_3 y_1) k$$
$$+ 2 x_3 x_4 \ (z_1 y_2 - y_1 z_2) i + 2 y_3 y_4 \ (x_1 z_2 - z_1 x_2) j + 2 z_3 z_4 \ (y_1 x_2 - x_1 y_2) k$$
$$= 2 (x_1 x_4 + y_1 y_4 + z_1 z_4) \left\{ (z_2 y_3 - y_2 z_3) i + (x_2 z_3 - z_2 x_3) j + (y_2 x_3 - x_2 y_3) k \right\}$$
$$- 2 x_1 x_4 \ (x_2 z_3 - z_2 z_3) j - 2 x_1 x_4 \ (y_2 x_3 - x_2 y_3) k - 2 y_1 y_4 \ (z_2 y_3 - y_2 z_3) i$$
$$- 2 y_1 y_4 \ (y_2 x_3 - x_2 y_3) k - 2 z_1 z_4 \ (z_2 y_3 - y_2 z_3) i - 2 z_1 z_4 \ (x_2 z_3 - z_2 x_3) j$$
$$+ 2 (x_2 x_4 + y_2 y_4 + z_2 z_4) \left\{ (z_3 y_1 - y_3 z_1) i + (x_3 z_1 - z_3 x_1) j + (y_3 x_1 - x_3 y_1) k \right\}$$
$$- 2 x_2 x_4 \ (x_3 z_1 - z_3 x_1) j - 2 x_2 x_4 \ (y_3 x_1 - x_3 y_1) k - 2 y_2 y_4 \ (z_3 y_1 - y_3 z_1) i$$
$$- 2 y_2 y_4 \ (y_3 x_1 - x_3 y_1) k - 2 z_2 z_4 \ (z_3 y_1 - y_3 z_1) i - 2 z_2 z_4 \ (x_3 z_1 - z_3 x_1) j$$
$$+ 2 (x_3 x_4 + y_3 y_4 + z_3 z_4) \left\{ (x_1 y_2 - y_1 z_2) i + (x_1 z_2 - z_1 x_2) j + (y_1 x_2 - x_1 y_2) k \right\}$$
$$- 2 x_3 x_4 \ (x_1 z_2 - z_2 x_2) j - 2 x_3 x_4 \ (y_1 x_2 - x_1 y_2) k - 2 y_3 y_4 \ (z_1 y_2 - y_1 z_2) i$$
$$- 2 y_3 y_4 \ (y_1 x_2 - x_1 y_2) k - 2 z_3 z_4 \ (z_1 y_2 - y_1 z_2) i - 2 z_3 z_4 \ (x_1 z_2 - z_1 x_2) j$$
$$= 2 (x_1 x_4 + y_1 y_4 + z_1 z_4) \left\{ (z_2 y_3 - y_2 z_3) i + (x_2 z_3 - z_2 x_3) j + (y_2 x_3 - x_2 y_3) k \right\}$$

$$+ 2(x_2 x_4 + y_2 y_4 + z_2 z_4)\{(z_3 y_1 - y_3 z_1)i + (x_3 z_1 - z_3 x_1)j + (y_3 x_1 - x_3 y_1)k\}$$

$$+ 2(x_3 x_4 + y_3 y_4 + z_3 z_4)\{(z_1 y_2 - y_1 z_2)i + (x_1 z_2 - z_1 x_2)j + (y_1 x_2 - x_1 y_2)k\}$$

$$= (\alpha\delta' + \delta\alpha')\prod_{\beta\gamma} + (\beta\delta' + \delta\beta')\prod_{\gamma\alpha} + (\gamma\delta' + \delta\gamma')\prod_{\alpha\beta},$$

or
$$\left(\gamma\prod_{\alpha\beta}' + \prod_{\alpha\beta}\gamma'\right)\delta = (\alpha\delta' + \delta\alpha')\prod_{\beta\gamma} + (\beta\delta' + \delta\beta')\prod_{\gamma\alpha} + (\gamma\delta' + \delta\gamma')\prod_{\alpha\beta}. \qquad (20)$$

By Formula (7)

$$\prod_{\alpha\beta} = (z_1 y_2 - y_1 z_2)i + (x_1 z_2 - z_1 x_2)j + (y_1 x_2 - x_1 y_2)k,$$

$$\prod_{\gamma\delta} = (z_3 y_4 - y_3 z_4)i + (x_3 z_4 - z_3 x_4)j + (y_3 x_4 - x_3 y_4)k;$$

consequently by the Formula (5)

$$\prod_{\alpha\beta}\prod_{\gamma\delta}' + \prod_{\gamma\delta}\prod_{\alpha\beta}'$$

$$= 2(z_1 y_2 - y_1 z_2)(z_3 y_4 - y_3 z_4)i + 2(x_1 z_2 - z_1 x_2)(x_3 z_4 - z_3 x_4)i + 2(y_1 x_2 - x_1 y_2)(y_3 x_4 - x_3 y_4)i;$$

on making the multiplications, and adding to the second side these three zeros: $x_1 x_2 x_3 x_4 - x_1 x_2 x_3 x_4$, $y_1 y_2 y_3 y_4 - y_1 y_2 y_3 y_4$, $z_1 z_2 z_3 z_4 - z_1 z_2 z_3 z_4$ we shall readily find

$$\prod_{\alpha\beta}\prod_{\gamma\delta}' + \prod_{\gamma\delta}\prod_{\alpha\beta}' = 2(x_1 x_3 + y_1 y_3 + z_1 z_3)(x x_2 + y y_2 + z z_2)i$$

$$- 2(x_1 x_4 + y_1 y_4 + z_1 z_4)(x_2 x_3 + y_2 y_3 + z_2 z_3)i,$$

or again by Formula (5)

$$\prod_{\alpha\beta}\prod_{\gamma\delta}' + \prod_{\gamma\delta}\prod_{\alpha\beta}'$$

$$= \tfrac{1}{2}(\beta\delta' + \delta\beta')(\alpha\gamma' + \gamma\alpha') - \tfrac{1}{2}(\alpha\delta' + \delta\alpha')(\beta\gamma' + \gamma\beta'). \qquad (21)$$

79. Examples.

Ex. 1. On the sides A B, A C of a triangle are constructed any two parallelograms A B D E, A C F G; the sides D E, F G are produced to meet in H. Prove that the sum of the areas of the parallelograms A B D E, A C F G is equal to the area of the parallelogram whose adjacent sides are respectively equal and parallel to B C and A H.

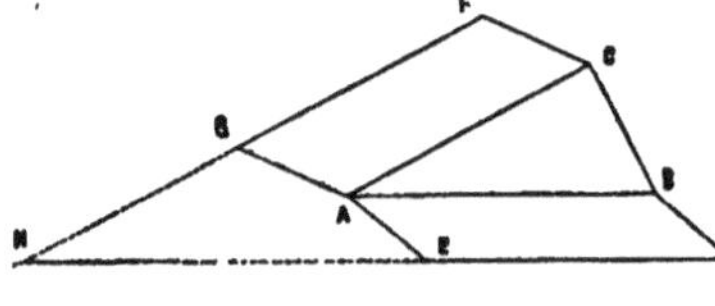

Let $AB = \alpha$, $AE = \beta$, $AC = \gamma$, $AG = \delta$, and $AH = \varepsilon$; then x and y indicating two numbers, $\varepsilon = \beta - x\alpha$, $\varepsilon = \delta - y\gamma$, and $BC = \gamma - \alpha$.

By Formula (8)

$$\prod_{\alpha\varepsilon} = \prod_{\alpha(\beta - x\alpha)} = \prod_{\alpha\beta} - \prod_{\alpha x\alpha} = \prod_{\alpha\beta} \quad \text{(Art (74)),}$$

and
$$\prod_{\gamma\varepsilon} = \prod_{\gamma(\delta-y\gamma)} = \prod_{\gamma\delta} - \prod_{\gamma y\gamma} = \prod_{\gamma\delta};$$

consequently
$$\prod_{\gamma\varepsilon} - \prod_{\alpha\varepsilon} = \prod_{\gamma\delta} - \prod_{\alpha\beta}$$

or
$$\prod_{(\gamma-\alpha)\varepsilon} = \prod_{\gamma\delta} + \prod_{\beta\gamma}.$$

Besides, the definition of the special perpendicular shows that each term of this equation has the same unit; we will represent it by u. We know that (Art. 69) the abstract number of $\prod_{(\gamma-\alpha)\varepsilon}$ is the area of the parallelogram whose adjacent sides are respectively equal and parallel to B C and A H; and the number of $\prod_{\gamma\delta}$ and $\prod_{\beta\alpha}$ are respectively the areas of the parallelograms A B F G, A O D E. We will represent the first of these three parallelograms by A; the second, by B, the third by G; hence

$$A\,u = B\,u + cu$$

or
$$(A - B - C)\,u = 0;$$

$$A - B - C = 0 \qquad \text{or} \qquad A = B + C.$$

The ordinary resolution of this problem is very simple.

Ex. 2. The squares of the sides of any quadrilateral exceed the squares of the diagonals by four times the square of the line which joins the middle points of the diagonals.

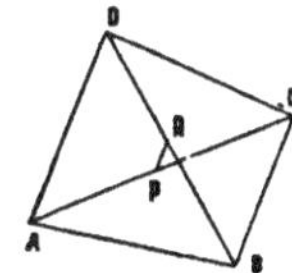

Let P, Q be the middle points of A C, B D; and let $AB = \alpha$, $AC = \beta$, $AD = \gamma$; then $BD = \gamma - \alpha$.

Therefore

$$PQ = AQ - AP = \frac{\alpha + \gamma}{2} - \frac{\beta}{2},$$

or
$$2\,PQ = \alpha + \gamma - \beta.$$

Hence the numerical equation that we can deduce is

$$4\,(PQ)^2 = \alpha^2 + \gamma^2 + \beta^2 + (\alpha\gamma' + \gamma\alpha') - (\alpha\beta' + \beta\alpha') - (\gamma\beta' + \beta\gamma) \qquad \text{(Formula (3))};$$

but
$$\alpha\gamma' + \gamma\alpha' = \alpha^2 + \gamma^2 - (BD)^2,$$

$$\alpha\beta' + \beta\alpha' = \alpha^2 + \beta^2 - (BC)^2,$$

$$\gamma\beta' + \beta\gamma' = \gamma^2 + \beta^2 - (CD)^2;$$

therefore
$$4\,(PQ)^2 = (AB)^2 + (BC)^2 + (DC)^2 + (AD)^2 - \{ (AC)^2 + (BD)^2 \}.$$

Ex. 3. Let
$$\alpha = x_1 i + y_1 j + z_1 k,$$
$$\beta = x_2 i + y_2 j + z_2 k.$$

We know that
$$\underline{\alpha}^2 = x_1^2 + y_1^2 + z_1^2, \quad \underline{\beta}^2 = x_2^2 + y_2^2 + z_2^2 ;$$

And
$$\underline{\alpha\beta' + \beta\alpha'} = 2(x_1 x_2 + y_1 y_2 + z_1 z_2),$$

$$N \prod_{\alpha\beta} = \sqrt{\left\{ (y_1 z_2 - z_1 y_2)^2 + (z_1 x_2 - x_1 z_2)^2 + (x_1 y_2 - y_1 x_2)^2 \right\}}.$$

Therefore, let us replace

$\underline{\alpha}^2$, $\underline{\beta}^2$, $\underline{\alpha\beta' + \beta\alpha'}$, $N\prod_{\alpha\beta}$ in the Formula (3) by their above equivalent, we shall at once have

$$(x_1^2 + y_1^2 + z_1^2)(x_2^2 + y_2^2 + z_2^2)$$
$$= (x_1 x_2 + y_1 y_2 + z_1 z_2)^2 + (y_1 z_2 - z_1 y_2)^2$$
$$+ (z_1 x_2 - x_1 z_2)^2 + (x_1 y_2 - y_1 x_2)^2.$$

Ex. 4. To find the volume of the pyramid of which the vertex is a given point, and the base the triangle formed by joining three given points on the *rectangular co-ordinate axis*.

Let A, B, C be the three given points; $OA = a$, $OB = b$, $OC = c$; x, y, z the three co-ordinates of the given point P. Then $OA = ai$, $OB = bj$, $OC = ck$; and $OP = xi + yj + zk$. Let $PA = \alpha$, $PB = \beta$, $PC = \gamma$; $V =$ the volume of the pyramid $PABC$.

Hence $\alpha = OA - OP = -(x-a)i - yj - zk;$
$$\beta = OB - OP = -xi - (y-b)j - zk,$$
$$\gamma = OC - OP = -xi - yj - (z-c)k.$$

By Formula (7)
$$\prod_{\alpha\beta} = \{ z(y-b) - yz \} i + \{ (x-a)z - xz) \} j + \{ xy - (x-a)(y-b) \} k$$
$$= -bzi - azj - (ab - ay - bx)k.$$

And (art. 74)
$$\gamma \prod_{\alpha\beta}' + \prod_{\alpha\beta} \gamma = 12\ Vi.$$

$$(-xi - yj - zk + ck)(-bzi + azj + abk - ayk - bxk)$$
$$+ (-bzi - azj - abk + ayk + bxk)(-xi + yj + zk - ck)$$
$$= 12\ Vi;$$

after having made the two multiplications which are in the first side, we shall find

$$6\,V = a\,b\,z + a\,c\,y + b\,c\,x - a\,b\,c,$$

or
$$V = \tfrac{1}{6}\,a\,b\,c \left(\frac{x}{a} + \frac{y}{b} + \frac{z}{c} - 1 \right).$$

If V prove to be negative, it will indicate that the pyramid $PABC$ is below the plane ABC.

Ex. 5. To express the relation between the sides of a spherical triangle and the angles opposite to them.

Retaining the notations and figure of Ex., Art. 68, we shall have,

$$\prod_{\alpha\beta} = \operatorname{Sin} c \cdot u_1 \, , \quad \prod_{\beta\gamma} = \operatorname{Sin} a \cdot u_2 \, ,$$

u_1 is the unit of the special perpendicular of α, β; and u_2 is the unit of the special perpendicular of β, γ. It is readily seen that the angle which is found between u_1 and u_2 is the supplement of the angle B of the spherical triangle ABC; and that OB or β is perpendicular to the plane which passes through u_1, u_2. Therefore

$$\prod_{\substack{\Pi \quad \Pi \\ \alpha\beta \quad \beta\gamma}} = - \operatorname{Sin} c \cdot \operatorname{Sin} a \cdot \operatorname{Sin} B \cdot \beta .$$

By Formula (1)

$$\alpha \prod_{\beta\gamma}' + \prod_{\beta\gamma} \alpha' = - 2 \operatorname{Sin} a \cdot \operatorname{Sin} \varphi \cdot i,$$

φ represents the angle which is between the line OA and the plane COB; therefore

$$\beta \left(\alpha \prod_{\beta\gamma}' + \prod_{\beta\gamma} \alpha' \right) = - 2 \operatorname{Sin} a \cdot \operatorname{Sin} \varphi \cdot \beta .$$

But by Formula (17)

$$\prod_{\substack{\Pi \, \Pi \\ \alpha\beta \, \beta\gamma}} = \tfrac{1}{2} \left(\alpha \prod_{\beta\gamma}' + \prod_{\beta\gamma} \alpha' \right) \beta = - \operatorname{Sin} a \cdot \operatorname{Sin} \varphi \cdot \beta ;$$

$$\operatorname{Sin} c \cdot \operatorname{Sin} a \cdot \operatorname{Sin} B = \operatorname{Sin} a \cdot \operatorname{Sin} \varphi ,$$

or
$$\operatorname{Sin} \varphi = \operatorname{Sin} c \cdot \operatorname{Sin} B .$$

Similarly
$$\operatorname{Sin} \varphi = \operatorname{Sin} b \cdot \operatorname{Sin} C .$$

Therefore
$$\operatorname{Sin} c \cdot \operatorname{Sin} B = \operatorname{Sin} b \cdot \operatorname{Sin} C ,$$

or
$$\operatorname{Sin} b : \operatorname{Sin} c :: \operatorname{Sin} B : \operatorname{Sin} C .$$

Ex. 6. To find the condition that the perpendiculars from the angles of a tetrahedron on the opposite faces shall intersect one onother.

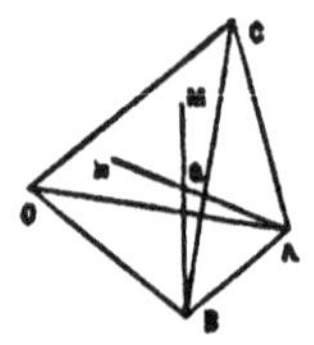

Let O A, O B, O C be the edges of the tetrahedron, and $OA = \alpha$, $OB = \beta$, $OC = \gamma$. Let the perpendiculars from A and B on the opposite faces, be A N, B M. We know that $NA = m \prod_{\gamma\beta}$ and $MB = n \prod_{\alpha\gamma}$ (Art. 70), m and n being two numbers; if these perpendiculars intersect in G, the three points A, B, G will be in one plane, and the special perpendicular of A N, B M will be perpendicular to the line $AB = \beta - \alpha$; and $mn \prod_{\prod_{\alpha\gamma} \prod_{\gamma\beta}}$ which is the special perpendicular of B M and A N (Art. 71) is found perpendicular to A B. Hence (Art. 65)

$$(\beta - \alpha) \prod'_{\prod_{\alpha\gamma} \prod_{\gamma\beta}} + \prod_{\prod_{\alpha\gamma} \prod_{\gamma\beta}} (\beta' - \alpha') = 0;$$

but by Formula (17)

$$\prod_{\prod_{\alpha\gamma} \prod_{\gamma\beta}} = \tfrac{1}{2} \left(\prod_{\alpha\gamma} \beta' + \beta \prod'_{\alpha\gamma} \right) \gamma;$$

therefore

$$(\beta - \alpha) \left(\prod_{\alpha\gamma} \beta' + \beta \prod'_{\alpha\gamma} \right) \gamma' + \left(\prod_{\alpha\gamma} \beta' + \beta \prod'_{\alpha\gamma} \right) \gamma \, (\beta' - \alpha') = 0,$$

or

$$\left(\prod_{\alpha\gamma} \beta' + \beta \prod'_{\alpha\gamma} \right) \mid (\beta - \alpha) \gamma' + \gamma \, (\beta' - \alpha') \mid = 0.$$

It is evident that, $\prod_{\alpha\gamma} \beta' + \beta \prod'_{\alpha\gamma}$ cannot be $= 0$. Therefore,

$$(\beta - \alpha) \gamma' + \gamma \, (\beta' - \alpha') = 0;$$

$$\therefore \quad \beta \gamma' + \gamma \beta' = \alpha \gamma' + \gamma \alpha';$$

but by Formula (1) $\quad \beta \gamma' + \gamma \beta' = (\underline{OB}^2 + \underline{OC}^2 - \underline{BC}^2) i$

and $\quad \alpha \gamma' + \gamma \alpha' = (\underline{OA}^2 + \underline{OC}^2 - \underline{AC}^2) i;$

$$\therefore \quad \underline{OB}^2 + \underline{OC}^2 - \underline{BC}^2 = \underline{OA}^2 + \underline{OC}^2 - \underline{AC}^2,$$

or $\quad OB^2 + \underline{AC}^2 = \underline{BC}^2 + \underline{OA}^2.$

Consequently the condition that all three perpendiculars shall meet in a point is that the sum of the squares of each pair of opposite edges shall be the same.

Ex. 7. Any point Q is joined to the angular points A, B, C, O of a tetrahedron, and the joining lines, produced if necessary, meet the opposite faces in a, b, c, o; to prove that

$$\frac{Qa}{Qa - QA} + \frac{Qb}{Qb - QB} + \frac{Qc}{Qc - QC} + \frac{Qo}{Qo - QO} = 1.$$

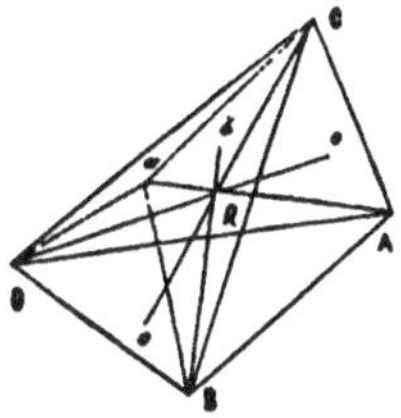

Let $\quad QA = \alpha, \; QB = \beta, \; QC = \gamma,$

$$QO = \delta; \; Qa = a\alpha, \; Qb = b\beta,$$

$$Qc = c\gamma, \; Qo = d\delta. \quad \text{Then}$$

$$AB = \beta - \alpha, \; AC = \gamma - \alpha, \; OB = \beta - \delta, \; OC = \gamma - \delta,$$

$$aO = \delta - a\alpha. \quad \text{Therefore}$$

$$(\delta - a\alpha) \prod'_{(\beta - \delta)\,(\gamma - \delta)} + \prod_{(\beta - \delta)\,(\gamma - \delta)} (\delta' - a\alpha') = 0,$$

or by Formula (8)

$$(\delta - a\alpha)\left(\prod'_{\beta\gamma} - \prod'_{\delta\gamma} - \prod'_{\beta\delta} + \prod'_{\delta\delta} \right)$$

$$+ \left(\prod_{\beta\gamma} - \prod_{\delta\gamma} - \prod_{\beta\delta} + \prod_{\delta\delta} \right)(\delta' - a\alpha') = 0,$$

or

$$a\alpha\left(\prod'_{\beta\gamma} + \prod'_{\gamma\delta} + \prod'_{\delta\beta} \right) + \left(\prod_{\beta\gamma} + \prod_{\gamma\delta} + \prod_{\delta\beta} \right)a\alpha'$$

$$- \left(\delta\prod'_{\beta\gamma} + \prod_{\beta\gamma}\delta' \right) - \left(\delta\prod'_{\gamma\delta} + \prod_{\gamma\delta}\delta' \right) - \left(\delta\prod'_{\beta\delta} + \prod_{\beta\delta}\delta' \right) = 0,$$

or $\; a\alpha\left(\prod'_{\beta\gamma} + \prod'_{\gamma\delta} + \prod'_{\delta\beta} \right) + \left(\prod_{\beta\gamma} + \prod_{\gamma\delta} + \prod_{\delta\beta} \right)a\alpha' - \left(\beta\prod'_{\gamma\delta} + \prod_{\gamma\delta}\beta' \right) = 0;$

$$\therefore \; a\left\{ \alpha\prod'_{\beta\gamma} + \alpha\prod'_{\gamma\delta} + \alpha\prod'_{\delta\beta} + \prod_{\beta\gamma}\alpha' + \prod_{\gamma\delta}\alpha' + \prod_{\delta\beta}\alpha' \right\} - \left(\beta\prod'_{\gamma\delta} + \prod_{\gamma\delta}\beta' \right) = 0.$$

We can find in the same way, that,

$$b\left\{ \beta\prod'_{\alpha\gamma} + \beta\prod'_{\gamma\delta} + \beta\prod'_{\delta\alpha} + \prod_{\alpha\gamma}\beta' + \prod_{\gamma\delta}\beta' + \prod_{\delta\alpha}\beta' \right\} - \left(\alpha\prod'_{\gamma\delta} + \prod_{\gamma\delta}\alpha' \right) = 0;$$

$$c\left\{ \gamma\prod'_{\alpha\beta} + \gamma\prod'_{\beta\delta} + \gamma\prod'_{\delta\alpha} + \prod_{\alpha\beta}\gamma' + \prod_{\beta\delta}\gamma' + \prod_{\delta\alpha}\gamma' \right\} - \left(\alpha\prod'_{\beta\delta} + \prod_{\alpha\delta}\alpha' \right) = 0;$$

$$d\left\{ \delta\prod'_{\alpha\beta} + \delta\prod'_{\beta\gamma} + \prod'_{\gamma\alpha} + \prod_{\alpha\beta}\delta' + \prod_{\beta\gamma}\delta' + \prod_{\gamma\alpha}\delta' \right\} - \left(\alpha\prod_{\beta\gamma} + \prod_{\beta\gamma}\alpha' \right) = 0.$$

Now if we write

$$\alpha\prod'_{\beta\gamma} + \prod_{\beta\gamma}\alpha' = xi, \quad \alpha\prod'_{\gamma\delta} + \prod_{\gamma\delta}\alpha' = yi, \quad \alpha\prod'_{\delta\beta} + \prod_{\delta\beta}\alpha' = zi,$$

$$\beta\prod'_{\gamma\delta} + \prod_{\gamma\delta}\beta' = wi,$$

and apply the Formulæ (9) and (2) we get

$$a x + a y + a z - \; w = 0,$$
$$-b x - y - b z + b \, w = 0,$$
$$c x + c y + z - c \, w = 0,$$
$$-x - d y - d z + d \, w = 0,$$

which give

$$\frac{a}{a-1}\, x + \frac{d}{d-1}\, w = 0,$$

$$\frac{a}{a-1}\, y + \frac{b}{b-1}\, w = 0,$$

$$\frac{c}{c-1}\, y - \frac{b}{b-1}\, z = 0,$$

$$\frac{c}{c-1}\, x - \frac{d}{d-1}\, z = 0;$$

and therefore,

$$\frac{1}{a-1} + \frac{b}{b-1} + \frac{c}{c-1} + \frac{d}{d-1} = 0,$$

or
$$\frac{a}{a-1} + \frac{b}{b-1} + \frac{c}{c-1} + \frac{d}{d-1} = 1;$$

but by supposition

$$a = \frac{Q\,a}{Q\,A}, \quad b = \frac{Q\,b}{Q\,B}, \quad c = \frac{Q\,c}{Q\,C}, \quad d = \frac{Q\,o}{Q\,O},$$

consequently

$$\frac{a}{a-1} = \frac{Q\,a}{Q\,a - Q\,A}, \quad \text{etc.};$$

therefore

$$\frac{Q\,a}{Q\,a - Q\,A} + \frac{Q\,b}{Q\,b - Q\,B} + \frac{Q\,c}{Q\,c - Q\,C} + \frac{Q\,o}{Q\,o - Q\,O} = 1.$$

CHAPTER IV.

Equation of a Straight Line.

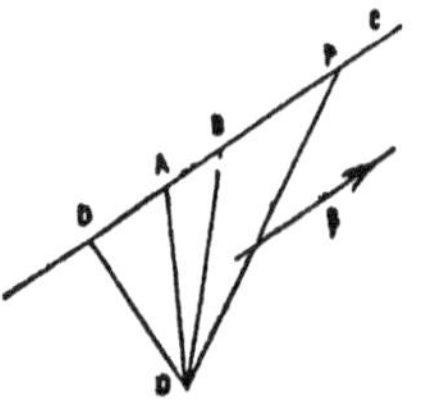

80. Let β be a line having the same direction as that of D C of which the equation is required; α the line from origin O to a given point A in the line D C; ρ that to any point P whatever in the same line from the same origin; then A P having the same direction as β is a multiple of this; let $A P = x \beta$; the equation $OP = OA + AP$

gives
$$\rho = \alpha + x \beta \tag{1}$$

as the equation of the line D C.

Another form in which the equation of a straight line may be expressed is this: instead of the direction of the line and the position of a point in it being given, let us suppose two points in the line to be given, and let $OA = \alpha$, $OB = \gamma$; then

$$AB = \gamma - \alpha \quad \text{and} \quad AP = x(\gamma - \alpha),$$

$$\rho = \alpha + x(\gamma - \alpha). \tag{2}$$

We can readily deduce the second equation from the first: we have only to suppose that β is $= \gamma - \alpha$.

A third form may be exhibited in which the perpendicular on the line DC from the origin is given.

Let OD perpendicular to $DC = \delta$;

then
$$DP = \rho - \delta$$

and
$$\delta(\rho' - \delta') + (\rho - \delta)\delta' = 0,$$

because δ is perpendicular to $(\rho - \delta)$;

then
$$\delta\rho' - \delta\delta' + \rho\delta' - \delta\delta' = 0,$$

$\therefore$
$$\rho\delta' + \delta\rho' = 2\delta\delta' = 2d^2 i, \tag{3}$$

where d^2 is a constant (Art. 64).

Equation of a plane.

81. Let P be any point in the plane of which the equation is required, OD perpendicular to the some plane; and let

$$OD = \delta, \quad OP = \rho;$$

then
$$\rho - \delta = DP,$$

which is in a direction perpendicular to OD;

$\therefore$
$$\delta(\rho' - \delta') + (\rho - \delta)\delta' = 0,$$

or
$$\delta\rho' + \rho\delta' = 2\delta^2 i.$$

If the plane pass through O, ρ can have the value zero,

$$\delta\rho' + \rho\delta' = 0 \text{ is the equation.}$$

Sice a line can be drawn in the plane through D, parallel to any given line in or parallel to the plane; if β be any line in or parallel to the plane,

$$\delta\beta' + \beta\delta' = 0.$$

82. To find the length of the perpendicular from a given point on a given plane.

7

Let
$$\delta \rho' + \rho \delta' = C \cdot i$$

be the equation of the plane, γ the line to the given point from the origin; then let the perpendicular line be $x\delta$, we have

$$\rho = \gamma + x\delta;$$

then
$$\rho \delta' = \gamma \delta' + x\delta \delta',$$

and
$$\delta \rho' = \delta \gamma' + x\delta \delta';$$

∴
$$\rho \delta' + \delta \rho' = \gamma \delta' + \delta \gamma' + 2x\delta^2 \cdot i = C \cdot i,$$

which gives
$$2x\delta^2 \cdot i = C \cdot i - (\gamma \delta' + \delta \gamma')$$

or
$$x\delta i = \frac{Ci - (\gamma \delta' + \delta \gamma')}{2\delta},$$

or
$$x\delta = \frac{C - N(\gamma \delta' + \delta \gamma')}{2\delta}.$$

Equation of a circle.

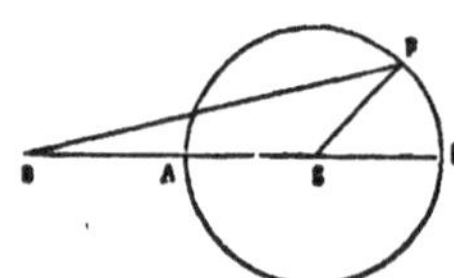

83. Let AD be the diameter of the circle, C the centre, and $a =$ the radius, and let P be any point. If O be the origin and $OP = \rho$, $OC = \gamma$, $CP = \rho - \gamma$.

We have

$$(\rho - \gamma)(\rho' - \gamma') = CP \cdot (CP)' = a^2 \cdot i \quad (\text{Art. } 64).$$

If $OC = c$, we can put this last equation in this form

$$\rho \rho' - (\rho \gamma' + \gamma \rho') = (a^2 - c^2) \cdot i.$$

The Sphere.

84. It is clear that there is nothing in the demonstration of Art. 83 which limits the conclusion to one plane; it follows that the equation there obtained is also the equation of a sphere.

The equation of a Conic Section deduced directly from its definition.

85. We will define a Conic Section as *the locus of a point which moves so that its distance from a fixed point bears a constant ratio to its distance from a fixed straight lens.* (Kelland and Tait, Art. 43).

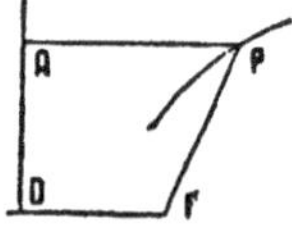

Let F be the given point, DQ the given straight line, $FP = e \, PQ$ the given relation, F, P, Q, D all in one plane. Let $FD = \alpha$, $FP = \rho$, $DQ = y\gamma$, γ being the unit line in the direction DQ, and $PQ = x\alpha$; then

$$\rho = e x \alpha,$$

thence
$$\rho^2 = e^2 x^2 \alpha^2;$$

but
$$\underline{\rho^2}\, i = \rho\,\rho', \text{ and } \underline{\alpha^2}\, i = \alpha\,\alpha' \quad \text{(Art. 64)}$$

then
$$\rho\,\rho' = e^2\, x^2\, \alpha\,\alpha',$$

and
$$\alpha\,\alpha'\, x^2 = \frac{\rho\,\rho'}{e^2}\;.$$

But
$$\rho + x\,\alpha = FD + DQ = \alpha + y\,\gamma\,;$$

$\therefore$
$$\rho\,\alpha' + x\,\alpha\,\alpha' = \alpha\,\alpha' + y\,\gamma\,\alpha',$$

and
$$\alpha\,\rho' + \alpha\,x\,\alpha' = \alpha\,\alpha' + \alpha'\,y\,\gamma\,.$$

Here
$$\alpha\,\rho' + \rho\,\alpha' + 2\,x\,\alpha\,\alpha' = 2\,\alpha\,\alpha',$$

for $\alpha\,\gamma' + \gamma\,\alpha' = 0$;

and
$$2\,x\,\alpha\,\alpha' = 2\,\alpha\,\alpha' - (\alpha\,\rho' + \rho\,\alpha'),$$

or
$$4\,x^2\,(\alpha\,\alpha')^2 = \{2\,\alpha\,\alpha' - (\alpha\,\rho' + \rho\,\alpha')\}^2;$$

hence
$$\frac{4\,\rho\,\rho'}{e^2}\,.\,\alpha\,\alpha' = \{2\,\alpha\,\alpha' - (\alpha\,\rho' + \rho\,\alpha')\}^2$$

or
$$\rho\,\rho'\,.\,\alpha\,\alpha' = e^2\{\alpha\,\alpha' - \tfrac{1}{2}(\alpha\,\rho' + \rho\,\alpha')\}^2, \qquad\qquad (1)$$

which is the required equation.

The Ellipse.

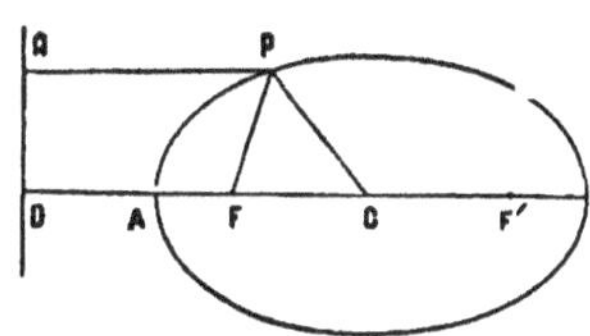

86. When e is less than 1, the Curve which the equation (1) represents is an ellipse. FA, FA, are multiples of α: Call ane of them $x\,\alpha$; then by equation (1) putting $x\,\alpha$ for ρ and therefore $x\,\alpha'$ for ρ', we get,

$$x^2\,\alpha\,\alpha'\,.\,\alpha\,\alpha' = e^2\{\alpha\,\alpha' - \tfrac{1}{2}(x\,\alpha\,\alpha' + x\,\alpha\,\alpha')\}^2$$

$$= e^2\{\alpha\,\alpha' - x\,\alpha\,\alpha'\}^2,$$

$$x^2 = e^2\,(1 - x)^2$$

$\therefore$

$$x = \pm\, e\,(1 - x);$$

or

hence
$$x = \frac{e}{1 + e}\,, \quad \text{or} \quad x = -\,\frac{e}{1 - e}\,.$$

Consequently,

$$\underline{FA} = \frac{e}{1 + e}\ \underline{FD}\,,$$

$$\underline{FA_1} = \frac{e}{1 - e}\ \underline{FD}\,;$$

$$\underline{A A_1} = \frac{2e}{1-e^2}\ \underline{FD},$$

the major axis of the ellipse, which we shall as usual abbreviate by $2\,a$.

If C be the centre of the ellipse,

$$\underline{FC} = \underline{FA_1} - \underline{CA_1} = \left(\frac{e}{1-e} - \frac{e}{1-e^2}\right)\underline{FD}$$

$$= \frac{e^2}{1-e^2}\ \underline{FD} = e \cdot \frac{e}{1-e^2}\ \underline{FD}$$

$$= e\,a;$$

and if the line CF be designated by β, CP by γ, we have

$$\beta = \frac{e^2}{1-e^2}\,\alpha,\ \text{ and }\ \gamma = \rho + \beta,$$

or

$$\alpha = \frac{1-e^2}{e^2}\,\beta,\ \text{ and }\ \rho = \gamma - \beta;$$

then

$$\alpha\rho' + \rho\alpha' = \frac{1-e^2}{e^2}\,\beta\,(\gamma - \beta') + (\gamma - \beta)\,\frac{1-e^2}{e^2}\,\beta'$$

$$= \frac{1-e^2}{e^2}\{(\beta\gamma' + \gamma\beta') - 2\beta\beta'\};$$

and

$$\alpha\alpha' = \frac{(1-e^2)^2}{e^4}\,\beta\beta',$$

also

$$\rho\rho' \cdot \alpha\alpha' = (\gamma - \beta)(\gamma' - \beta')\,\frac{(1-e^2)^2}{e^4}\,\beta\beta'$$

$$= \frac{(1-e^2)^2}{e^4}\Big[\beta\beta' \cdot \gamma\gamma' + (\beta\beta')^2 - (\gamma\beta' + \beta\gamma')\beta\beta'\Big];$$

whence, by substituting in (1), and remembering that $\beta\beta' = e^2 a^2 . i$, the equation assumes the form

$$(\beta\gamma' + \gamma\beta')^2 - 4a^2\gamma\gamma' = -4a^4(1-e^2)i;$$

which we may now write, CF being α and CP ρ,

$$(\alpha\rho' + \rho\alpha')^2 - 4a^2\rho\rho' = -4a^4(1-e^2)i. \qquad (2)$$

From this last equation we can have

$$i = \frac{2a^2\rho\rho' - \frac{1}{4}(\alpha\rho' + \rho\alpha')^2}{2a^4(1-e^2)}$$

$$= \frac{2a^2\rho\rho' - \frac{1}{4}(\alpha\rho' + \rho\alpha')(\alpha\rho' + \rho\alpha')}{2a^4(1-e^2)}$$

$$= \frac{a^2\rho\rho' + a^2\rho\rho' - \frac{1}{4}(\alpha\rho' + \rho\alpha')\alpha\rho' - \frac{1}{4}(\alpha\rho' + \rho\alpha')\rho\alpha'}{2a^4(1-e^2)}$$

$$= \frac{a^2\rho - \frac{1}{2}(\alpha\rho'+\rho\alpha')\alpha}{2a^4(1-e^2)}\rho' + \rho\,\frac{a^2\rho'-\frac{1}{2}(\alpha\rho'+\rho\alpha')\alpha'}{2a^4(1-e^2)} \,;$$

if now we write $\Phi\rho$ for $\dfrac{a^2\rho - \frac{1}{2}(\alpha\rho'+\rho\alpha')\alpha}{2a^4(1-e^2)}$ where $\Phi\rho$ is a line which coincides with ρ only in the cases in which either α coincides with ρ or when $\alpha\rho'+\rho\alpha'=0$; the equation of the ellipse becomes.

$$\rho \cdot \overset{\frown}{\Phi\rho'} + \Phi\rho \cdot \rho' = i. \tag{3}$$

From a simple inspection of the value of $\Phi\rho$

$$= \frac{a^2\rho - \frac{1}{2}(\alpha\rho'+\rho\alpha')\alpha}{2a^4(1-e^2)}$$

we see the following properties of $\Phi\rho$;

I. $\Phi(\rho+\sigma)=\Phi\rho+\Phi\sigma.$

II. $\Phi(x\rho)=x \cdot \Phi\rho.$

III. $\sigma \cdot \overset{\frown}{\Phi\rho'} + \Phi\rho \cdot \sigma' = \rho \cdot \overset{\frown}{\Phi\sigma'} + \Phi\sigma \cdot \rho'.$

The Hyperbola.

87. The same equation is, of course, applicable to the hyperbola, e being greater than 1.

The Parabola.

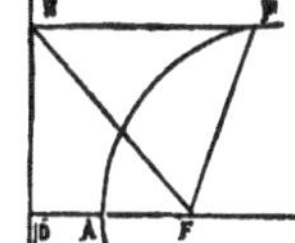

88. When $e=1$, that is $\overline{FP}=\overline{PQ}$, the curve which the equation (1) (Art. 85) represents is a $\overline{parabola}$. We have

$$\rho\rho \cdot \alpha\alpha' = \{\alpha\alpha' - \tfrac{1}{2}(\alpha\rho'+\rho\alpha')\}^2.$$

Hence

$$\rho\rho' \cdot \alpha\alpha' = (\alpha\alpha')^2 - \alpha\alpha' \cdot (\alpha\rho'+\rho\alpha') + \tfrac{1}{4}(\alpha\rho'+\rho\alpha')^2;$$

and, since $\alpha\alpha'=a^2 \cdot i$ (Art. 64),

$$i = \frac{4\rho\rho' \cdot \alpha\alpha' + 4\alpha\alpha'(\alpha\rho'+\rho\alpha') - (\alpha\rho'+\rho\alpha')^2}{4\alpha^4}$$

$$= \rho\,\frac{2\rho' \cdot \alpha'\alpha - (\alpha\rho'+\rho\alpha')\alpha' + 4\alpha\alpha' \cdot \alpha'}{4\alpha^4} + \frac{2\rho \cdot \alpha\alpha' - (\alpha\rho'+\rho\alpha')\alpha + 4\alpha'\alpha \cdot \alpha}{4\alpha^4}\rho'.$$

If now we write

$$\Phi\rho = \frac{2\rho \cdot \alpha\alpha' - (\alpha\rho'+\rho\alpha')\alpha}{4\alpha^4}$$

to which the properties of $\Phi\rho$ in Art. 86 evidently apply, the equation becomes

$$\rho\left\{\Phi\rho' + \frac{\alpha'}{\alpha^2}\right\} + \left\{\Phi\rho + \frac{\alpha}{\alpha^2}\right\}\rho' = i.$$

The Cone of Revolution.

89. Let the vertex of it be the origin. Suppose α, where $\alpha = 1$, to be along its axis, and e the cosine of its semi-vertical angle; then if ρ be the line from the origin to any point on the surface of the cone, and $u\rho$, the unit of ρ,

$$\alpha \cdot u\rho' + u\rho \cdot \alpha' = \pm 2 e\, i,$$

and

$$(\alpha \cdot u\rho' + u\rho \cdot \alpha')^2 = 4 e^2 i;$$

then

$$(\alpha \cdot u\rho' + u\rho \cdot \alpha')^2 \rho^2 = 4 e^2 \cdot \rho\rho',$$

or

$$(\alpha \cdot u\rho' \cdot \rho + u\rho \cdot \alpha' \rho)^2 = 4 e^2 \cdot \rho\rho';$$

therefore,

$$(\alpha\rho' + \rho\alpha')^2 = 4 e^2 \cdot \rho\rho'$$

is the required equation.

The Cone which has a Circular Section.

90. Suppose the vertex to be the origin, and let the circular section be the intersection of the plane

$$\alpha\rho' + \rho\alpha' = 2i$$

with the sphere (passing through the origin)

$$\rho\rho' = \tfrac{1}{2}(\beta\rho' + \rho\beta'),$$

α, β being two units of line.

These equations may be written thus

$$\rho \cdot (\alpha \cdot u\rho' + u\rho \cdot \alpha') = 2i,$$

$$\rho i = \tfrac{1}{2}(\beta \cdot u\rho' + u\rho \cdot \beta');$$

therefore, eliminating ρ, we find the following equation which $u\rho$ must satisfy,

$$\tfrac{1}{2}(\beta \cdot u\rho' + u\rho \cdot \beta')(\alpha \cdot u\rho' + u\rho \cdot \alpha') = 2i.$$

Hence

$$\rho^2 (\beta \cdot u\rho' + u\rho \cdot \beta')(\alpha \cdot u\rho' + u\rho \cdot \alpha') = 4\rho^2 i;$$

$$\therefore \quad (\beta\rho' + \rho\beta')(\alpha\rho' + \rho\alpha') = 4\rho\rho',$$

or

$$4\rho\rho' - (\beta\rho' + \rho\beta')(\alpha\rho' + \rho\alpha') = 0.$$

Now if $x\rho$ be written in place of ρ, the equation is not changed, it is therefore the required equation of the Cone.

As α and β are similarly involved, the mere form of this equation proves the existence of the sub-contrary section discovered by Appollonius. (Tait Art. 239).

CHAPTER V.

On some Additional Applications.

91. Let us designate by $f_1(t)$, $f_2(t)$, $f_3(t)$ ...... diverse *functions* of *one* indeterminate number, and by $f_1(t, u)$, $f_2(t, u)$, ... diverse functions of *two* indeterminate numbers. Let α_1, α_2, α_3 ...... be given lines; following the nature of the functions $f_1(t)$, $f_2(t)$ ......, $f_1(t, u)$, $f_2(t, u)$ ...... the equation

$$\rho = \alpha_1 f_1(t) + \alpha_2 f_2(t) + \ldots \ldots$$

may represent a *right line* or a *curve*, and the equation

$$\rho = \alpha_1 f_1(t+u) + \alpha_2 f_2(t+u) + \ldots \ldots$$

a *plane* or a *surface*.

The first equation is often written under one of these forms:

$$\rho = \Sigma \alpha f(t) \quad \text{and} \quad \rho = \Phi(t);$$

the second equation,

$$\rho = \Sigma \alpha f(t+u) \quad \text{and} \quad \rho = \Phi(t+u).$$

92. If P is a point on the curve that

$$\rho = \Sigma \alpha f(t)$$

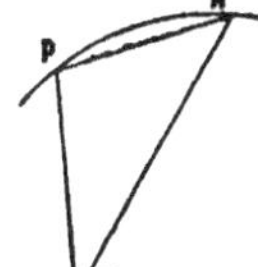

represents, $OP = \rho_1 = \alpha_1 f_1(t) + \alpha_2 f_2(t) + \ldots \ldots$ and similarly, if Q is any other point on the curve,

$$OQ = \rho_2 = \alpha_1 f_1(t + \Delta t) + \alpha_2 f_2(t + \Delta t) + \ldots \ldots$$

where Δt is any number whatever.

The line PQ is therefore

$$\rho_2 - \rho_1 = \Delta \rho_1 = \alpha_1 [f_1(t + \Delta t) - f_1(t)] + \alpha_2 [f_2(t + \Delta t) - f_2(t)] + \ldots \ldots$$

$$\frac{\Delta \rho_1}{\Delta t} = \alpha_1 \frac{f_1(t + \Delta t) - f_1(t)}{\Delta t} + \alpha_2 \frac{f_2(t + \Delta t) - f_2(t)}{\Delta t} + \ldots \ldots$$

and

$$\frac{d \rho_1}{d t} = \alpha_1 \frac{d f_1(t)}{d t} + \alpha_2 \frac{d f_2(t)}{d t} + \ldots \ldots$$

We can represent this result by

$$\frac{d \rho}{d t} = \Sigma \alpha \frac{d f(t)}{d t} \quad \text{or} \quad \frac{d \rho}{d t} = \frac{d \Phi(t)}{d t}.$$

Let OP be

$$\rho_1 = \Phi(t),$$

and OQ

$$\rho_2 = \Phi(t + \Delta t).$$

Let us suppose that the number t represents the *time*, and Δt is the *interval* of time that a point *moving along the curve* takes to come from P to Q. $\rho_2 - \rho_1$ or $\Phi(t + \Delta t) - \Phi t$, represents the line P Q. It is evident that $\frac{PQ}{\Delta t}$ or $\frac{\Delta \rho_1}{\Delta t}$ can represent the *average velocity* of a point which passes from P to Q on the line PQ, in the interval of Δt; it is also evident that when Q approaches nearer and nearer to P, that is to say, when Δt becomes smaller, the average velocity represented by $\frac{\Delta \rho}{\Delta t}$ approaches also more and more to the actual velocity at the point P of the point which describes the curve; therefore $\frac{d\rho}{dt}$ or $\frac{d\Phi(t)}{dt}$ is the velocity of this point when it is at P; that is to say, if the point which describes the curve arrived at the point P ceases to be accelerated in departing from the point P, it will continue to move on the tangent at the point P with the velocity $\frac{d\rho}{dt}$; this expression represents not only absolute value of velocity but its direction as well.

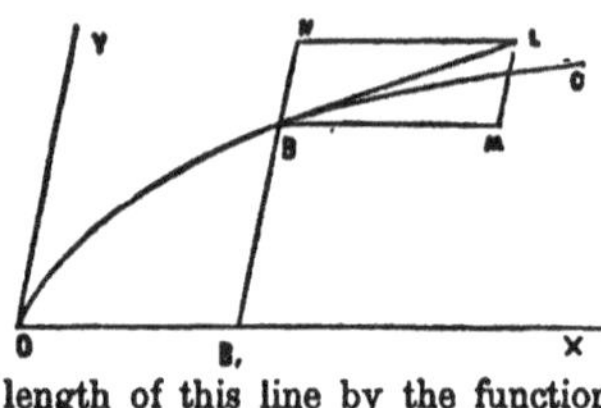

93. Example. Let us suppose that a point moves from O to X on the line OX, conformably to this equation $x = f(t)$, x being the space passed over, and t the time; let us also suppose that another point moves along the curve OBC in such a manner that the line which joins this point to the point which describes the line OX, shall have constantly the same direction as OY; we will represent the length of this line by the function $F(x)$.

To find the velocity of the point which, comformably to the conditions above laid down describes the curve OBC.

The equation of this curve may be written thus,

$$\rho = x\,\alpha + F(x)\,\beta,$$

α being the unit of the direction OX; β that of the direction OY.

Therefore

$$\frac{\Delta \rho}{\Delta t} = \frac{\Delta x}{\Delta t}\,\alpha + \frac{F(x + \Delta x) - F(x)}{\Delta x} \cdot \frac{\Delta x}{\Delta t}\,\beta$$

$$\frac{d\rho}{dt} = \frac{dx}{dt}\,\alpha + \frac{dF(x)}{dx} \cdot \frac{dx}{dt}\,\beta .$$

This equation shows that the course travelled over on the line OX being OB,, if we describe the line BM equal to the velocity at the point B,, and the line BN which has the direction OY and the length $\frac{dF(x)}{dx} \cdot \frac{dx}{dt}$, we shall have the velocity at the point $B = BM + BN = BL.$

To find the absolute value of this velocity $\frac{d\rho}{dt}$ we have only to multiply it by $\frac{d\rho'}{dt}$, the product will be the square of its absolute value $\times i$ (Art. 64).

Suppose that OY being perpendicular to OX we have

$$x = v_0 \cos \theta \cdot t,$$

and
$$F(x) = x \cdot \tan \theta - \frac{g}{2 v_0^2 \cos^2 \theta} \, x^2.$$

Then the equation of the curve will be,

$$\rho = x i + \left(x \tan \theta - \frac{g}{2 v_0^2 \cos^2 \theta} \cdot x^2 \right) j,$$

O X being the principal direction.

These equations give,

$$\frac{d\rho}{dt} = \frac{dx}{dt} \left\{ i + \left(\tan \theta - \frac{g\,x}{v_0^2 \cos^2 \theta} \right) j \right\}$$

and
$$\frac{dx}{dt} = v_0 \cos \theta.$$

Consequently,

$$\frac{d\rho}{dt} = v_0 \cos \theta \cdot i + (v_0 \sin \theta - g \cdot t) j$$

is the velocity at the end of the time t.

To have the absolute value of this velocity, let us multiply it by

$$\frac{d\rho'}{dt} = v_0 \cos \theta \cdot i - (v_0 \sin \theta - g\,t) j,$$

we shall find

$$\frac{d\rho}{dt} \cdot \frac{d\rho'}{dt} = N^2 \left(\frac{d\rho}{dt} \right) \cdot i$$

$$= \left| v_0^2 \cos^2 \theta + (v_0 \sin \theta - g\,t)^2 \right| i$$

$$= \left| v_0^2 - 2 v_0 \sin \theta \cdot g\,t + g^2 t^2 \right| i.$$

It is unnecessary to observe that an example of this nature is given for illustration merely.

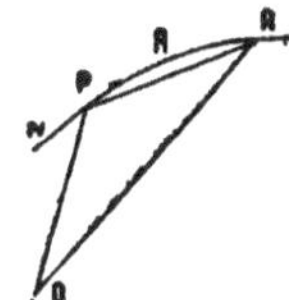

94. Let us suppose that a curve is represented by

$$\rho = \Sigma \alpha f(t),$$

and that s being the length of this curve mesaured from some fixed point is
$$t = \varphi(s);$$

then
$$\rho = \Sigma \alpha f(\varphi(s)) \text{ or } \rho = \Sigma \alpha F(s).$$

The last equation gives

$$\Delta \rho = \rho_2 - \rho_1 = \Sigma \alpha F(s + \Delta s) - \Sigma \alpha F(s) = PQ,$$

O P being ρ_1, O Q ρ_2.

Thus

$$\frac{\Delta \rho}{\Delta s} = \Sigma \alpha \frac{F(s + \Delta s) - F(s)}{\Delta s};$$

$$\frac{d\rho}{ds} = \Sigma\alpha\,\frac{d\,F(s)}{d\,s} = \frac{d\,\Phi(s)}{d\,s}$$

must be a linear unit in the direction of the tangent at the extremity P of ρ_2, for evidently $\mathcal{L}\dfrac{\Delta\dot\rho}{arc\,PQ} = 1$.

At the proximate point, denoted by $s+\Delta s$ this linear unit tangent becomes

$$\frac{d\,(\rho+\Delta\rho)}{d\,s} = \Sigma\alpha\,\frac{d\,F(s+\Delta s)}{d\,s}\,.$$

But $F(s+\Delta s)$ is by Taylor's theorm equal to

$$F(s) + \frac{d\,F(s)}{d\,s}\,\Delta s + \frac{d^2\,F(s)}{d\,s^2}\,\frac{(\Delta s)^2}{1\,.\,2} + \ldots\ldots$$

hence

$$\frac{d\,(\rho+\Delta\dot\rho)}{d\,s} = \Sigma\alpha\,\frac{d\,F(s)}{d\,s} + \Sigma\alpha\,\frac{d^2\,F(s)}{d\,s^2}\,\Delta s + \Sigma\alpha\,\frac{d^3\,F(s)}{d\,s^3}\,\frac{(\Delta s)^2}{1\,.\,2} + \ldots\ldots$$

$$= \frac{d\,\Phi(s)}{d\,s} + \frac{d^2\,\Phi(s)}{d\,s^2}\,\Delta s + \frac{d^3\,\Phi(s)}{d\,s^3}\,\frac{(\Delta s)^2}{1\,.\,2} + \ldots\ldots$$

Now if we designate the conjugate of $\Sigma\alpha\dfrac{d\,F(s)}{d\,s}$ by $\Sigma\alpha'\dfrac{d\,F(s)}{d\,s}$ or $\dfrac{d\,\Phi'(s)}{d\,s}$, and if we multiply this equation by its conjugate, we shall have

$$\frac{d\,(\rho+\Delta\rho)}{d\,s}\,.\,\frac{d\,(\rho'+\Delta\rho')}{d\,s}$$

$$= \frac{d\,\Phi(s)}{d\,s}\,.\,\frac{d\,\Phi'(s)}{d\,s} + \frac{d^2\,\Phi(s)}{d\,s^2}\,\Delta s\,.\,\frac{d\,\Phi'(s)}{d\,s} + \ldots\ldots$$

$$+ \frac{d\,\Phi(s)}{d\,s}\,.\,\frac{d^2\,\Phi'(s)}{d\,s^2}\,\Delta s + \frac{d^2\,\Phi(s)}{d\,s^2}\,\Delta s\,.\,\frac{d^2\,\Phi'(s)}{d\,s^2}\,\Delta s + \ldots\ldots$$

$$+ \ldots\ldots\ldots\ldots\ldots\ldots\ldots\ldots\ldots\ldots$$

But we know that

$$\frac{d\,(\rho+\Delta\rho)}{d\,s}\,.\,\frac{d\,(\rho'+\Delta\rho')}{d\,s} = i \text{ or } 1\,,$$

and

$$\frac{d\,\Phi(s)}{d\,s}\,.\,\frac{d\,\Phi'(s)}{d\,s} = i \text{ or } 1 \quad \text{(Art. 64)};$$

hence

$$\frac{d^2\,\Phi(s)}{d\,s^2}\,.\,\frac{d\,\Phi'(s)}{d\,s}\,\Delta s + \ldots\ldots + \frac{d\,\Phi s}{d\,s}\,.\,\frac{d^2\,\Phi'(s)}{d\,s^2}\,\Delta s + \ldots\ldots = 0\,;$$

by dividing this on Δs and afterwards by making $\Delta s = 0$ we shall find

$$\frac{d^2\,\Phi(s)}{d\,s^2}\,.\,\frac{d\,\Phi'(s)}{d\,s} + \frac{d\,\Phi(s)}{d\,s}\,.\,\frac{d^2\,\Phi'(s)}{d\,s^2} = 0\,.$$

Hence $\dfrac{d^2\Phi(s)}{ds^2}$ or $\Sigma\alpha\,\dfrac{d^2 F(s)}{ds^2}$ is a line in the osculating plane of the curve, and perpendicular to the tangent $\dfrac{d\Phi(s)}{ds}$ or $\Sigma\alpha\,\dfrac{d F(s)}{ds}$.

95. If $\Delta\theta$ is the angle between the successive tangents $\dfrac{d\Phi(s)}{ds}$ and

$$\frac{d\Phi(s)}{ds}+\frac{d^2\Phi(s)}{ds^2}\cdot\Delta s+\ldots\ldots$$

and if $\dfrac{d\Phi(s)}{ds}$ is represented by $PP_{,}$, $\dfrac{d\,\Phi(s+\Delta s)}{ds}$ by $QQ_{,}$; and lastly if $QP_{,,}=PP_{,,}$,

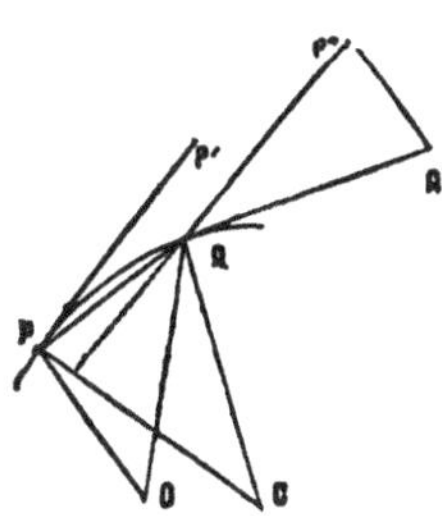

we shall have

$$P_{,,}Q=QQ_{,}-QP_{,,}$$

$$=\frac{d^2\Phi(s)}{ds^2}\,\Delta s+\frac{d^3\Phi(s)}{ds^3}\frac{(\Delta s)^2}{1\cdot2}+\ldots\ldots$$

Besides $\underline{QQ_{,}}=\underline{QP_{,,}}=1$; the angle $Q_{,}QP_{,,}$ being extremely small we can suppose $\underline{P_{,,}Q_{,}}=\Delta\theta$; if C is the centre of curvature at P, PQ or Δs being very small we can consider the triangles $Q_{,}QP_{,,}$, QCP similar. Hence

$$\underline{P_{,,}Q_{,}}=\Delta\theta=N\left\{\frac{d^2\Phi(s)}{ds^2}\cdot\Delta s+\frac{d^3\Phi(s)}{ds^3}\cdot\frac{(\Delta s)^2}{1\cdot2}+\ldots\ldots\right\}$$

or

$$\frac{\Delta\theta}{\Delta s}=N\left\{\frac{d^2\Phi(s)}{ds^2}+\frac{d\Phi^3(s)}{ds^3}\cdot\frac{(\Delta s)^2}{1\cdot2}+\ldots\ldots\right\}\cdot$$

Therefore

$$\mathcal{L}\,\frac{\Delta\theta}{\Delta s}=\frac{d\theta}{ds}=N\frac{d^2\Phi(s)}{ds^2},$$

but as the triangles $Q_{,}QP_{,,}$, QCP at the limit become similar

$$\mathcal{L}\,\frac{\Delta\theta}{\Delta s}=\frac{1}{\underline{R}},$$

R being radius CP of absolute curvature at the point P.

Hence

$$N\frac{d^2\Phi(s)}{ds^2}=\frac{1}{\underline{R}}$$

or

$$\underline{R}=\frac{1}{N\dfrac{d^2\Phi(s)}{ds^2}};$$

so that the number of $\dfrac{d^2\Phi(s)}{ds^2}$ is the reciprocal of the radius of absolute curvature at the point P, to which point s is corresponding.

96. We have seen that the line $\dfrac{d^2 \Phi(s)}{ds^2}$ is perpendicular to the tangent, and that it is in the osculating plane, thus $\dfrac{d^2 \Phi(s)}{ds^2}$ must be on the same line as R. Then

$$R = \underline{R} \cdot U \frac{d^2 \Phi(s)}{ds^2}.$$

Besides

$$U \frac{d^2 \Phi(s)}{ds^2} = \frac{\dfrac{d^2 \Phi(s)}{ds^2}}{N \dfrac{d^2 \Phi(s)}{ds^2}},$$

consequently

$$R = \frac{\dfrac{d^2 \Phi(s)}{ds^2}}{N^2 \dfrac{d^2 \Phi(s)}{ds^2}}.$$

97. Thus, if $OP = \Phi(s)$ is the line from the origin O to any point P of the curve, and if C is the centre of curvature at P, we have $PC = R$, and $OC = OP + PC$

$$= \Phi(s) + \frac{\dfrac{d^2 \Phi(s)}{ds^2}}{N^2 \dfrac{d^2 \Phi(s)}{ds^2}}$$ is the equation of the locus of the centre of the curvature.

98. Hence also $\prod_{\frac{d\Phi(s)}{ds} \frac{d^2 \Phi(s)}{ds^2}}$ is perpendicular to the osculating plane; and the unit of this line may be represented by

$$\frac{\prod}{\dfrac{d\Phi(s)}{ds} U \dfrac{d^2 \Phi(s)}{ds^2}},$$

then

$$N \frac{d \prod_{\frac{d\Phi(s)}{ds} U \frac{d^2 \Phi(s)}{ds^2}}}{ds}$$

or

$$N \prod_{\frac{d}{ds}\left(\frac{d\Phi(s)}{ds} U \frac{d^2 \Phi(s)}{ds^2}\right)}$$

is the *tortuosity* of the given curve, or the rate of rotation of its osculating plane per unit of length. (Tait. Art. 283).

99. Ex. 1. Let

$$\rho = \alpha t + \beta \frac{t^2}{2},$$

where t is an indeterminate number, and α, β given lines. The curve which this equation represents is evidently a parabola. See Tait. Art. 288.

Here
$$\frac{d\rho}{ds} = (\alpha + \beta t)\frac{dt}{ds},$$

and
$$\frac{d^2\rho}{ds^2} = (\alpha + \beta t)\frac{d^2 t}{ds^2} + \beta\left(\frac{dt}{ds}\right)^2,$$

whence, if we assume $\alpha\beta' + \beta\alpha' = 0$,
$$\left(\frac{dt}{ds}\right)^2 (\alpha\alpha' + \beta\beta' t^2) = i,$$

or
$$\left(\frac{dt}{ds}\right)^2 = \frac{i}{\alpha\alpha' + \beta\beta' t^2};$$

and
$$\frac{dt}{ds} = (\alpha\alpha' + \beta\beta' t^2)^{-\frac{1}{2}}.$$

$$\frac{d^2 t}{ds^2} = -\frac{\beta\beta' t}{(\alpha\alpha' + \beta\beta' t^2)^{\frac{3}{2}}} \cdot \frac{dt}{ds} = -\frac{\beta\beta' t}{(\alpha\alpha' + \beta\beta' t^2)^2};$$

$$\frac{d^2\rho}{ds^2} = -(\alpha + \beta t)\cdot\frac{\beta\beta' t}{(\alpha\alpha' + \beta\beta' t^2)^2} + \beta\frac{i}{\alpha\alpha' + \beta\beta' t^2}$$

$$= \frac{\beta\cdot\alpha\alpha' - \alpha\cdot\beta\beta' t}{(\alpha\alpha' + \beta\beta' t^2)^2};$$

and
$$N^2\frac{d^2\rho}{ds^2} = \frac{\beta^2\alpha^4 + \alpha^2\beta^4 t^2}{(\alpha^2 + \beta^2 t^2)^4} = \frac{\alpha^2\cdot\beta^2}{(\alpha^2 + \beta^2 t^2)^3};$$

hence
$$R = \frac{(\alpha^2 + \beta^2 t^2)^{\frac{3}{2}}}{\alpha\cdot\beta}.$$

Therefore, for the locus of the centre of curvature
$$\omega = OC = \alpha t + \beta\frac{t^2}{2} + \frac{(\alpha^2 + \beta^2 t^2)(\beta\cdot\alpha^2 - \alpha\beta^2 t)}{\alpha^2\cdot\beta^2}$$

$$= \beta\left(\frac{3 t^2}{2} + \frac{\alpha\alpha'}{\beta\beta'}\right) - \alpha\frac{\beta\beta'}{\alpha\alpha'}\cdot t^2;$$

which is the linear equation of the *evolute*.

100. Ex. 2. To find the curve whose curvature and tortuosity are both constant. Tait. Art. 284.

We have
$$\text{curvature} = N\frac{d^2\Phi(s)}{ds^2} = c$$

and
$$\text{tortuosity} = \frac{N\Pi}{\frac{d}{ds}\left[\frac{d\Phi(s)}{ds}U\frac{d^2\Phi(s)}{ds^2}\right]} = c_1,$$

or
$$N\frac{d^2\rho}{ds^2}=c \qquad \text{and} \quad N\prod_{\frac{d}{ds}\left(\frac{d\rho}{ds}U\frac{d^2\rho}{ds^2}\right)}=c_1.$$

Hence
$$N\frac{d^2\rho}{ds^2}\cdot\prod_{\frac{d\rho}{ds}U\frac{d^2\rho}{ds^2}}=\prod_{\frac{d\rho}{ds}N\frac{d^2\rho}{ds^2}\cdot U\frac{d^2\rho}{ds^2}}$$

$$=\prod_{\frac{d\rho}{ds}\frac{d^2\rho}{ds^2}}=c\alpha,$$

where α is a unit line perpendicular to the osculating plane, that is $\alpha=\prod\limits_{\frac{d\rho}{ds}U\frac{d^2\rho}{ds^2}}$

This gives
$$\prod_{\frac{d}{ds}\left(\frac{d\rho}{ds}\frac{d^2\rho}{ds^2}\right)}=c\,\mathcal{L}\frac{\Delta\alpha}{ds}=cc_1\,U\frac{d^2\rho}{ds^2}=c_1\frac{d^2\rho}{ds^2}.$$

Integrating we get
$$\prod_{\frac{d\rho}{ds}\frac{d^2\rho}{ds^2}}=c_1\frac{d\rho}{ds}+\beta, \qquad\qquad (1)$$

where β is a constant line. From this,
$$c^2\alpha\alpha'=c_1^2\,i+\beta\beta'+c_1\left(\frac{d\rho}{ds}\beta'+\beta\frac{d\rho'}{ds}\right),$$

and
$$0=2c_1\,i+\beta\frac{d\rho'}{ds}+\frac{d\rho}{ds}\beta';$$

then
$$\underline{\beta^2}=c^2+c_1^2.$$

And also
$$\prod_{\frac{d\rho}{ds}\prod_{\frac{d\rho}{ds}\frac{d^2\rho}{ds^2}}}=\prod_{\frac{d\rho}{ds}\left(c_1\frac{d\rho}{ds}+\beta\right)}=\prod_{c_1\frac{d\rho}{ds}\frac{d\rho}{ds}+\frac{d\rho}{ds}\beta}=\prod_{\frac{d\rho}{ds}\beta};$$

but
$$\prod_{\frac{d\rho}{ds}\prod_{\frac{d\rho}{ds}\frac{d^2\rho}{ds^2}}}=-\frac{d^2\rho}{ds^2},$$

$$\frac{d^2\rho}{ds^2}=-\prod_{\frac{d\rho}{ds}\beta},$$

or by integrating
$$\frac{d\rho}{ds} = -\prod_{\rho\,\beta} + \omega,$$

where ω is a constant line. Eliminating $\frac{d\rho}{ds}$, we get

$$\frac{d^2\rho}{ds^2} = -\prod_{(-\prod_{\rho\beta}+\omega)\beta} = \prod_{\prod_{\rho\beta}\beta} - \prod_{\omega\beta}.$$

But $\displaystyle\prod_{\rho\beta} = \underline{\rho}\underline{\beta} \sin\theta \cdot \epsilon$, from this $\displaystyle\prod_{\prod_{\rho\beta}\beta} = \underline{\rho}\underline{\beta}^2 \sin\theta \cdot \epsilon$,

where θ is the angle between ρ, β transferred to the same origin; and ϵ is a unit line perpendicular to β and being on the plane passing through ρ, β. Evidently

$$\epsilon = \frac{\cos\theta}{\sin\theta}\, \mathrm{U}\beta - \frac{1}{\sin\theta}\, \mathrm{U}\rho.$$

We have
$$\frac{d\rho}{ds}\beta' + \beta\frac{d\rho'}{ds} = -2c_1 i,$$
or by integration
$$\rho\beta' + \beta\rho' = -2c_1 si + 2ai = 2\underline{\rho}\underline{\beta}\cos\theta \cdot i,$$

where $2a$ is a constant number; hence

$$\cos\theta = -\frac{c_1 s}{\underline{\rho}\underline{\beta}} + \frac{a}{\underline{\rho}\underline{\beta}}.$$

$$\prod_{\prod_{\rho\beta}\beta} = \underline{\rho}\underline{\beta}^2\left(-\frac{c_1 s}{\underline{\rho}\underline{\beta}} + \frac{a}{\underline{\rho}\underline{\beta}}\right)\mathrm{U}\beta - \underline{\rho}\underline{\beta}^2\,\mathrm{U}\rho$$

$$= -c_1 s\beta + a\beta - \underline{\beta}^2\rho;$$

$$\frac{d^2\rho}{ds^2} = -c_1 s\beta + a\beta - \underline{\beta}^2\rho - \prod_{\omega\beta},$$

or
$$\frac{d^2\rho}{ds^2} + \underline{\beta}^2\rho = -c_1 s\beta + a\beta - \prod_{\omega\beta}.$$

The complete integral of this equation is
$$\rho = \xi\cos.\underline{\beta}s + \eta\sin.\underline{\beta}s - \frac{1}{\underline{\beta}^2}\left(c_1 s\beta - a\beta + \prod_{\omega\beta}\right), \qquad (a)$$

ξ and η being any two constant lines.
From this we have

$$\beta\rho' + \rho\beta' = (\beta\xi' + \xi\beta')\cos.\underline{\beta}s + (\beta\eta' + \eta\beta')\sin.\underline{\beta}s - 2c_1 si + 2ai$$

or
$$(\beta\xi' + \xi\beta')\cos.\underline{\beta}s + (\beta\eta' + \eta\beta')\sin.\underline{\beta}s = 0,$$

which requires that
$$\beta\xi' + \xi\beta' = 0, \qquad \beta\eta' + \eta\beta' = 0;$$

also we have

$$\frac{d\rho}{ds} = -\xi \underline{\beta} \sin . \underline{\beta} s + \eta \underline{\beta} \cos . \underline{\beta} s - \frac{c_1 \underline{\beta}}{\underline{\beta}^2},$$

and

$$\frac{d\rho'}{ds} = -\xi' \underline{\beta} \sin . \underline{\beta} s + \eta' \underline{\beta} \cos . \underline{\beta} s - \frac{c_1 \underline{\beta}'}{\underline{\beta}^2},$$

therefore, remembering that $N \left(\frac{d\rho}{ds} \cdot \frac{d\rho'}{ds} \right) = 1$,

$$1 = \underline{\xi}^2 \underline{\beta}^2 \sin^2 . \underline{\beta} s + \underline{\eta}^2 \underline{\beta}^2 \cos^2 . \underline{\beta} s - (\underline{\eta \xi' + \xi \eta'}) \underline{\beta}^2 \sin . \underline{\beta} s \cos . \underline{\beta} s + \frac{c_1^2}{\underline{\beta}^2}.$$

This requires, of course,

$$\eta \xi' + \xi \eta' = 0, \qquad \underline{\xi} = \underline{\eta} = \frac{\sqrt{\underline{\beta^2 - c_1^2}}}{\underline{\beta}^2} = \frac{c}{c^2 + c_1^2},$$

so that (a) becomes the general equation of a helix traced on a right cylinder.

⁓⁓⁓⁓⁓

APPENDIX.

Complex Quantities and Quaternions.

We can add a *linear equality* with a *numerical* one. For example, let

$$\alpha = \gamma + \delta,$$

$$n = a + b;$$

we can write,

$$\alpha + n = \gamma + \delta + a + b,$$

or

$$\alpha + n = a + b + \delta + \gamma,$$

and

$$\alpha + n = a + \delta + b + \gamma.$$

Such an equality will always be correct with the conditions

$$\alpha = \gamma + \delta$$

$$n = a + b.$$

We can multiply a linear equality by a numerical equality or *vice versa*. For example, let

$$\alpha = \gamma + \delta,$$

$$n = a + b;$$

we can write,

$$n\alpha = (a + b)(\gamma + \delta)$$

or

$$n\alpha = (\gamma + \delta)(a + b);$$

and in effecting the multiplication

$$n\alpha = a\gamma + b\gamma + a\delta + b\delta$$

$$= \gamma a + \delta a + \gamma b + \delta b,$$

it is evident that this result is correct.

We can also multiply two complex equations by each other. For example, q and r being two complex quantities, let

$$q = \alpha + n = n + \gamma + \delta,$$

$$r = \beta + m = m + \rho + \omega;$$

we can write,

$$q \cdot r = (\alpha + n)(\beta + m) = (n + \gamma + \delta)(m + \rho + \omega)$$

or

$$\alpha\beta + n\beta + m\alpha + nm$$

$$= nm + m\gamma + m\delta$$

$$+ n\rho + \gamma\rho + \delta\rho \qquad (a)$$

$$+ n\omega + \gamma\omega + \delta\omega;$$

it is readily seen that this result is correct with the conditions,

$$\alpha = \gamma + \delta,$$

$$\beta = \rho + \omega,$$

which are the same conditions as those of the equalities given.

The equality (a) is the sum of these three equalities,

$$nm = nm,$$

$$m\alpha + n\beta = m\gamma + m\delta + n\rho + n\omega,$$

$$\alpha\beta = \gamma\rho + \gamma\omega + \delta\rho + \delta\omega;$$

and as from the last of these three equalities, we can deduce two others (Art. 78) we can deduce from the equality (a) four equalities,

I.
$$nm = nm$$

II.
$$c(\alpha\beta' + \beta\alpha') = c(\gamma\rho' + \rho\gamma') + c(\gamma\acute\omega + \omega\gamma') + c(\delta\rho' + \rho\delta') + c(\delta\acute\omega + \omega\delta'),$$

III.
$$n\beta + m\alpha = m\gamma + m\delta + n\rho + n\omega,$$

IV.
$$\prod_{\alpha\beta} = \prod_{\gamma\rho} + \prod_{\gamma\omega} + \prod_{\delta\rho} + \prod_{\delta\omega}.$$

In the second equality we have introduced the numerical factor c *for convenience.*

If we add these four equalities, we shall have a new complex equality. Let us designate the new complex quantity thus found, by $q \frown r$, that is to say

$$q \frown r = nm + c(\alpha\beta' + \beta\alpha') + m\alpha + n\beta + \prod_{\alpha\beta}, \qquad (1)$$

or

$$q \frown r = nm + c(\gamma\rho' + \rho\gamma') + c(\gamma\dot{\omega} + \omega\gamma') + c(\delta\rho' + \rho\delta') + c(\delta\dot{\omega} + \omega\delta') \qquad (2)$$

$$+ m\gamma + m\delta + n\rho + n\omega$$

$$+ \prod_{\gamma\rho} + \prod_{\gamma\omega} + \prod_{\delta\rho} + \prod_{\delta\omega}.$$

If we designate $n + \alpha$ by q, we will designate $n - \alpha$ by Kq; n being a number, and α a line.

Let

$$q = n + \alpha, \qquad\qquad r = m + \beta,$$

$$Kq = n - \alpha, \qquad\qquad Kr = m - \beta;$$

we shall have by multiplication

$$q \cdot Kq = n^2 - \alpha^2 \qquad \text{and} \qquad r \cdot Kr = m^2 - \beta^2.$$

Therefore

$$q \frown Kq = n^2 - 2c\underline{\alpha^2}, \qquad\qquad r \frown Kr = m^2 - 2c\underline{\beta^2};$$

consequently,

$$(q \frown Kq) \times (r \frown Kr) = n^2 m^2 - 2cn^2\underline{\beta^2} - 2cm^2\underline{\alpha^2} + 4c^2\underline{\alpha^2}\underline{\beta^2},$$

or

$$(q \frown Kq) \frown (r \frown Kr) = n^2 m^2 - 2cn^2\underline{\beta^2} - 2cm^2\underline{\alpha^2} + 4c^2\underline{\alpha^2}\underline{\beta^2}. \qquad (3)$$

Let us take again the proposed equalities,

$$q = n + \alpha, \qquad\qquad r = m + \beta,$$

by multiplication,

$$qr = nm + m\alpha + n\beta + \alpha\beta;$$

from this equation we can deduce,

$$q \frown r = nm + c(\alpha\beta' + \beta\alpha') + m\alpha + n\beta + \prod_{\alpha\beta},$$

and

$$k(q \frown r) = nm + c(\alpha\beta' + \beta\alpha') - m\alpha - n\beta - \prod_{\alpha\beta}; \qquad (4)$$

consequently, remembering that, $(\alpha\beta' + \beta\alpha')$ is a number,

$$(q \frown r) \times K(q \frown r) = n^2 m^2 + 2cnm(\alpha\beta' + \beta\alpha') - m^2\alpha^2 - n^2\beta^2$$

$$- nm\beta\alpha - nma\beta - m\alpha \prod_{\alpha\beta} \beta - n\alpha \prod_{\alpha\beta} \beta$$

$$+ c^2(\alpha\beta' + \beta\alpha')^2 - n\beta \coprod_{\alpha\beta} - m\alpha \prod_{\alpha\beta} - \prod_{\alpha\beta} \prod_{\alpha\beta};$$

Therefore
$$(q \frown r) \frown K(q \frown r) = n^2 m^2 + 2cnm(\alpha\beta' + \beta\alpha') - 2cm^2\alpha^2$$

$$- 2cn^2\beta^2 - 2cnm(\beta\alpha' + \alpha\beta')$$

$$+ c^2(\alpha\beta' + \beta\alpha') - 2c \, N^2 \prod_{\alpha\beta}$$

$$= n^2 m^2 - 2cm^2\alpha^2 - 2cn^2\beta^2$$

$$+ c^2(\alpha\beta' + \beta\alpha')^2 - 2c \, N^2 \prod_{\alpha\beta}. \qquad (5)$$

In subtracting from this equation (5), equation (3) we shall have

$$(q \frown r) \frown K(q \frown r) - (q \frown K q) \frown (r \frown K r) = c^2(\alpha\beta' + \beta\alpha')^2 - 2c \, N^2 \prod_{\alpha\beta} - 4c^2\alpha^2\beta^2. \quad (6)$$

In comparing the second side of this equation (6) with the second side of the equation
$$\alpha^2\beta^2 = \tfrac{1}{4}(\alpha\beta' + \beta\alpha')^2 + N^2 \prod_{\alpha\beta}$$ (Art. 78) we perceive that, taking $c = -\tfrac{1}{2}$, we have

$$c^2(\alpha\beta' + \beta\alpha)^2 - 2c \, N^2 \prod_{\alpha\beta} - 4c^2\alpha^2\beta^2 = 0.$$

Consequently, with the condition $c = -\tfrac{1}{2}$,

$$(q \frown r) \frown K(q \frown r) - (q \frown K q) \frown (r \frown K r) = 0 \text{ or } (q \frown r) \frown K(q \frown r) = (q \frown K q) \frown (r \frown K r). \quad (7)$$

Were the time and inclination to pursue this investigation which is extremely fruitful in curious results, at command, it would be seen that there are other advantages in the supposition $c = -\tfrac{1}{2}$.

Example.

Let
$$q = w_1 + \alpha = w_1 + x_1 i + y_1 j + z_1 k,$$

$$r = w_2 + \beta = w_2 + x_2 i + y_2 j + z_2 k;$$

and
$$K q = w_1 - \alpha = w_1 - x_1 i - y_1 j - z_1 k,$$

$$K r = w_2 - \beta = w_2 - x_2 i - y_2 j - z_2 k.$$

With the condition $c = -\tfrac{1}{2}$,
$$q \frown K q = w_1^2 + \alpha^2 = w_1^2 + x_1^2 + y_1^2 + z_1^2,$$

$$r \cap K\, r = w_2^2 + \beta^2 = w_2^2 + x_2^2 + y_2^2 + z_2^2;$$

$$(q \cap K\, q) \cap (r \cap K\, r) = (w_1^2 + x_1^2 + y_1^2 + z_1^2)(w_2^2 + x_2^2 + y_2^2 + z_2^2);$$

besides
$$-\tfrac{1}{2}(\alpha\beta' + \beta\alpha') = -(x_1 x_2 + y_1 y_2 + z_1 z_2),$$

$$\prod_{\alpha\beta} = (z_1 y_2 - y_1 z_2)i + (x_1 z_2 - z_1 x_2)j + (y_1 x_2 - x_1 y_2)k;$$

consequently,

$$q \cap r = w_1 w_2 - (x_1 x_2 + y_1 y_2 + z_1 z_2) + w_2(x_1 i + y j_1 + z_1 k)$$

$$+ w_1(x_2 i + y_2 j + z_2 k) + (z_1 y_2 - y_1 z_2)i + (x_1 z_2 - z_1 x_2)j$$

$$+ (y_1 x_2 - x_1 y_2)k,$$

or

$$q \cap r = (w_1 w_2 - x_1 x_2 - y_1 y_2 - z_1 z_2)$$

$$+ (w_2 x_1 + w_1 x_2 + z_1 y_2 - y_1 z_2)i$$

$$+ (w_2 y_1 + w_1 y_2 + x_1 z_2 - z_1 x_2)j$$

$$+ (w_2 z_1 + w_1 z_2 + y_1 x_2 - x_1 y_2)k.$$

Thus we can readily find, that,

$$(w_1^2 + x_1^2 + y_1^2 + z_1^2)(w_2^2 + x_2^2 + y_2^2 + z_2^2)$$

$$= (w_1 w_2 - x_1 x_2 - y_1 y_2 - z_1 z_2)^2 + (w_2 x_1 + w_1 x_2 + z_1 y_2 - y_1 z_2)^2$$

$$+ (w_1 y_1 + w_2 y_2 + x_1 z_2 - z_1 x_2)^2 + (w_2 z_1 + w_1 z_2 + y_1 x_2 - x_1 y_2)^2,$$

a formula of *numerical* algebra due to Euler. (Tait, Art. 103).

www.ingramcontent.com/pod-product-compliance
Lightning Source LLC
La Vergne TN
LVHW010657200726
843507LV00011B/1917